The Haunting of Blackstone Mansion

The Blackstone Trilogy Book 1
Augustine Pierce

Pierce Publishing

 Get your free book, *Zoe's Haunt*, by joining Augustine Pierce's newsletter. You can unsubscribe at any time.

Copyright © 2023 by Augustine Pierce

All rights reserved.

No portion of this book may be reproduced in any form without written permission from the publisher or author, except as permitted by U.S. copyright law.

Contents

Dedication	VII
1	1
2	8
3	26
4	39
5	55
6	75
7	85
8	101
9	111
10	126
11	145
12	153
13	166
14	178
15	194

16	216
17	231
18	242
19	254
20	270
21	287
22	293
The Possession of Blackstone Mansion	311
Acknowledgments	314
Dark Realm	315
Also by Augustine Pierce	316
About the Author	317

For Mom

1

"It's a fake," Katherine said with complete confidence. She knew the dark-chocolate-colored music box currently held out before her was a fake the instant she saw it, but she'd had to put on a bit of a show to demonstrate her expertise so that her client, Ms. Paulson, wouldn't simply dismiss her opinion.

Katherine was in her late thirties, tall and thin; too thin, according to her late mother, and wore jeans and a jean jacket, both of which were far too informal for her line of work—antiques—but she couldn't be bothered to class it up. Not anymore.

She was standing in a former drawing room, now show-room, of a bright and airy Victorian. The walls were a tasteful cream with a lavender fleur-de-lis pattern. Two huge display cases stood against each wall. They contained dozens of antique music boxes of various shapes, sizes, and styles. All were very rare, if not unique, in pristine condition, and therefore very expensive.

AUGUSTINE PIERCE

"I beg your pardon," the short man complained. He was dressed in a dark gray pinstripe suit and bowler hat. He stood to Katherine's right and was already turning red with frustration. Or maybe it was embarrassment now that she'd called him out.

He had a tired face, likely from years of hiding from all the scams he'd pulled on people. His hat covered a thinning scalp. Katherine suspected he wore it solely to lend an air of vintage authority to his demeanor.

She'd never understood why some men wore concealing headwear. *We can all see it's going. Why try to hide it?*

She had to fight not to roll her sea-blue eyes. "I said it's a fake. Want me to repeat it in Spanish? Greek? Latvian? Actually, scratch that. My Latvian's pretty much crap."

"I'm sorry, I don't understand." Ms. Paulson stood across from her. She was in her mid-thirties, a little on the short side, a little on the portly side.

Katherine could see that Ms. Paulson was deeply disappointed, but didn't want to lie to the woman and allow this jerk to make a quick twenty grand.

"It's not a goddamn fake!" The man stomped his foot. The music box tipped, but he managed to maintain a secure hold.

"Are you quite sure, Ms. Norrington?" Ms. Paulson's eyes darted between Katherine and the man.

THE HAUNTING OF BLACKSTONE MANSION

"No, she's not frickin' sure, 'cause it's not a fake!" the man declared.

Katherine threw a glance to her right, inviting Ms. Paulson to join her. Katherine held up a finger to the man. "One sec."

"Anything you're gonna say to her, you can say to me," the man complained.

Katherine ignored him. She and Ms. Paulson walked away a few steps. Katherine spoke in a low tone: "I understand you've been looking for this type of piece."

"For ages!" Ms. Paulson confirmed.

"Did you tell him that?"

"Yes, of course. Why? Should I not have?"

Great, so he can smell your desperation. "Gimme one sec."

Ms. Paulson returned to stand with the man.

Katherine sighed. "Here we go." She spun back around to face them. It was admittedly an attempt at a dramatic flourish, which didn't fully succeed, as several locks of her long, wavy raven hair stuck to her nose, so she had to quickly flick them off before she could continue.

She took a breath. "Yes, it is a goddamn fake. One, the lacquer trim was obviously done recently. As evidenced by the color—purple? Seriously?"

"It's lavender!" the man protested. "Same as the wallpaper!" He pointed at the opposite wall.

AUGUSTINE PIERCE

"It's birthday-balloon purple, if it's anything. That particular shade wasn't even available until 1933. Two, the outer wood shell, mahogany, is laughable as the shipping cost to the manufacturer in Chicago alone would've made the price of such an item in the mid-nineteenth century only conceivable to the wealthiest oil magnates, so, for the rest of us mortals, they would've had to have gone with green ash or black cherry. Three... May I?" She held out her hand.

The man glanced at Ms. Paulson as if he needed her permission, then passed the music box to Katherine.

"Thank you," she continued. "Three..." She turned the music box over and pointed out its manufacturer's plate. "While the Blythe family was indeed famous for their luxury music boxes, as you can see here, Ms. Paulson"—she pointed to the manufacturer's name, Blythe and Co.—"that's a typo. Or, 'engrave-o.' Should be Blythe and Sons." She lowered the music box and looked Ms. Paulson dead in the eyes. "Blythe and Sons *never* made engrave-os. Four..."

The man dropped all pretense of defensiveness. His tone was very dryly deadpan. "You've made your point, Ms. Norrington."

Katherine chuckled. "Oh, I'm just gettin' warmed up! Four, the ornamentation? He said it was original?" She pointed her thumb at the man. "If you look really close at the seam around where the silver meets the mahogany"—she tipped the music box ninety degrees toward Ms. Paulson, showing off the lid's in-laid silver floral pattern—"you can see these tiny little etchings where the wood was, well, recut." She lowered the music box to flat on her palms. "Somebody probably screwed up the initial measurements."

The man let out an impatient sigh.

"Almost done," Katherine assured him. "Now, the coup de grâce." She opened the box. It began to play some old weepy, tinkly tune. "Huh. Yeah, what I thought." She closed the lid. "It's playing a rendition of 'Good Night, My Sweet,' a very popular song, especially in the Chicago area, but written seven years *after* he claimed this piece was manufactured. And"—she opened the box again, listening intently to a few bars—"it's off-key. Blythe and Sons never would've let an off-key box out of their workshop." She handed the music box back to the man. "Oh, and I totally forgot! Look at the side?"

Ms. Paulson peered at the side of the music box.

"The crank?" Katherine asked.

"Used for winding it up!" the man declared.

"Not introduced till 1865. When did he say it dated from?"

"Eighteen forty-eight," Ms. Paulson said.

AUGUSTINE PIERCE

"Had it been made then, would've had a key." Katherine twisted an imaginary key to emphasize her point.

"Well, I've heard just about enough. You'll be hearing from my attorneys," Ms. Paulson spat at the man.

"Attorneys?" The man cackled derisively. "On what grounds?"

"Attempt to defraud me!"

"You can't be serious."

"That's not the half of it," Katherine interjected. "The suit? Notice the slight sheen reflecting the room's light? Ninety-ten wool and rayon blend doesn't do that. What's your blend? Seventy-five to twenty-five? At least?"

"I don't, uh..." The man trailed off.

"And the hat? Notice how the roundness isn't quite hemispherical? Just a little bit off?"

Ms. Paulson leaned in for a closer look. The man stepped back, probably uncomfortable with such scrutiny.

"Manufacturer probably used a cheap stiffener so it didn't fully hold," Katherine concluded.

The man grunted, looked like he might toss out some final insult at Katherine, but instead simply stormed out.

THE HAUNTING OF BLACKSTONE MANSION

"Thank you, Ms. Norrington," Ms. Paulson smiled wide at Katherine, "for saving me twenty thousand dollars."

"All in a day's work." Katherine tipped her own imaginary bowler hat. "Now, if you'll excuse me, I have a plane to catch." She headed out.

"Where do I send your check?"

Katherine didn't turn around. "PayPal. My account name's my e-mail address."

2

"Where the hell am I?" Katherine asked herself, the road, the unending sea of enormous, lush, verdant trees, and her Bluetooth-connected phone.

In the back seat sat a sole carry-on suitcase which contained all her worldly possessions, mainly clothes. She'd packed for her move with one rule: if it wasn't necessary or didn't fit in the suitcase, she didn't take it with her. That included dishes, a small collection of vinyl, and a few mementos, like framed pictures of family. The fact was that her move was intended to sever all ties, especially the nostalgic ones, with her life in New York.

She'd gone straight to the airport from Ms. Paulson's, taken a six-hour flight, and gotten on the road immediately on arrival at Portland International. She'd now been driving for what felt like another six hours, though, according to her phone's clock, it had only been about an hour and twenty.

THE HAUNTING OF BLACKSTONE MANSION

"Are you, uh, asking me? And if you are, are you being rhetorical?" a friendly male voice asked through the rental car's speakers.

"I have literally no idea where I am."

"You mean literally as in figuratively or literally as in—?"

"Sh, Dean, gimme a sec."

"Roger."

She sighed out loud.

"Are there any landmarks?" he asked.

"Do trees count?"

"Um..."

"'Cause this neck of the woods is stupid with the trees."

He laughed out loud. "Neck of the woods."

"Yeah, pun intended."

"I mean, you are in rural Oregon, Kitten."

"I know that." She hated that he called her Kitten. She used to love it, especially since it was such a stretch from Katherine, but now?

"Did I mention 'rural'?"

"Yeah, yeah." She checked the GPS of her rental. "Says I'm in the right—"

A carved wooden sign flashed right by.

"Damn it. Just missed it," she said.

"Missed what?"

"The sign."

"The sign for what?"

"The town? I dunno."

"Can you flip a bitch? Do they allow that in Oregon?"

"Stop saying Oregon as if it were some backward foreign country."

"I mean, if the shoe fits."

She checked her mirrors. No one was coming. "Not pullin' a U-ie. Just gonna retreat." She slowed to a stop, but hesitated. The world around her was suddenly very quiet.

His concerned voice popped over the speakers. "Kitten, you gotta explain it to me again. Why Blackstone?"

"You know why."

"I know I know why. But... why?"

"I had to get away."

"I know, but why not at least Portland? An actual city? Civilization? They've got beer and hippies and stuff."

"I don't need a city. I need isolation."

"But, I mean, there's isolation and there's bottom-of-the-mountain, middle-of-the-woods, serial-killer, Leatherface, *Deliverance* isolation."

"I know. And I appreciate your concern, but I need this right now." She reversed back to the sign. It was carved from a dark wood, with pleasant-looking, rounded letters that read Welcome to Blackstone, Oregon. "Yes!"

THE HAUNTING OF BLACKSTONE MANSION

"You found it?"

"Looks like it." She kept on her way, slower now, so she didn't miss anything else, like another sign or turnoff to another road.

"Right on! Ooh, tell me what the town's like."

"You'll just make fun of it. And me."

"I will not!" There was a long pause from the speakers. "Okay, maybe a little."

She soon came to a smattering of buildings, mostly houses. "I think I'm here."

"And? What's it like?"

She shrugged. "Small."

The buildings grew more frequent, and she realized that she was now in Blackstone's downtown area. She soon came upon a tree-lined town square. She pulled to a stop at a corner and took a second to admire the view.

Beyond the square stood more of Blackstone's houses and other buildings. They became more scattered until they gave way to the forests of Mt. Hood's foothills. It was a truly majestic, beautiful site. The exact image that photographers slapped on postcards.

A car horn honked behind her. She waved behind her at a pickup truck. "Sorry!"

"Did you fall asleep?" Dean asked.

"No, I did *not* fall asleep."

AUGUSTINE PIERCE

She found a parking spot around the corner of the square. She parked, removed her phone from the dashboard, stuck in her earbuds, and jumped out.

"So?" he asked over the earbuds.

"So what?"

"You gonna show me?"

"Here you go." She held up her phone and turned on video.

"Oh my God," he cooed.

"Stop." She grinned.

"Kitten, that is the most darling, little *Murder She Wrote* town I have ever..."

"Stop. *MSDub* is our, uh, I dunno. Fairview, Connecticut? Which is so much bigger than here, so your whole comparison kinda fails."

"So darling."

"Just what I need."

"Well, you're there now, so what's next?"

"That is a good question. Think I should find someplace to eat."

"All right, Kitten. You do that."

"Call you soon."

"Lates."

She hung up, took out her earbuds, stuffed her phone in her pocket, took in a deep breath, and gave Blackstone a 360 slow turn. Dean was right. It did look exactly like a postcard.

THE HAUNTING OF BLACKSTONE MANSION

The bell hanging from the diner's door rang with a disjointed, bouncing clang. Katherine eased the door shut as if that would quiet the tiny, ferocious, metallic beast. The diner had a U-shaped counter at which sat a dozen truckers. A handful of tables fanned out from the counter. A few heads turned to look at her, but then immediately lost interest.

She found a seat at the counter a few empty chairs away from the next customer. She picked up the little paper menu and skimmed for the least-disgusting thing. *Scrambled eggs and hot cocoa. Per-fect.*

"What can I get you, hon?" The server's name tag said Wendy. She was probably only in her early forties, but looked much older after probably decades of doing this kind of crap work, and who knew how much drinking and sucking on Marlboro Lights?

Katherine wasn't exactly one to judge. She was known to knock back a few now and again, but she thankfully did not look like that and hoped she never would. "Doorbell has a nice airy ring. A Declan Brothers bronze?"

Wendy shook her head. "I dunno. Sorry."

Katherine shrugged. "Just curious. Um, scrambled eggs would be great. And hot chocolate?"

"Whipped cream?"

"Uh, no, thanks."

"Comin' right up, hon."

"Thanks." Katherine looked outside, at the view of the town square. She grinned at the too-perfect notion that Blackstone's diner sat right on the square's southern edge. *Talk about postcard.*

She took out her phone and looked at the Google Map of the local area. "Grocery store, check. Bar, check. Hm. Apartments? Retail space?" She switched gears, dinking around on Facebook. She went straight for Dean's profile. Picture after picture of a delighted gay man living his best, late-thirties life. Most also contained his equally joyful, just as handsome husband, Ryan. They had selfies of them skiing, parasailing, and tearing it up at Mardi Gras on Bourbon Street in New Orleans.

"Here you go, hon." Wendy placed Katherine's eggs and hot cocoa in front of her.

"Thank you," Katherine said a little too eagerly. She dug in. She must have been very hungry. *Oh my God, this is the best pile of scrambled eggs I've ever had! What did they put in this? Sea salt and cocaine?*

She must have been making lots of noise as she slurped down her eggs because Wendy paused nearby and cocked a skeptical eyebrow. "Good?"

"Huh? Oh yeah, sorry, uh, yes, and I haven't eaten since this morning."

Wendy nodded.

THE HAUNTING OF BLACKSTONE MANSION

Katherine took a big gulp of the hot cocoa. She had always had a love-hate relationship with cocoa. She'd become a connoisseur early in life at Girl Scout campouts, had been spoiled on a semester abroad to Paris, but had also gotten so desperate in her poorer, non-Parisian college days that she'd pathetically resorted to Swiss Miss.

This hot cocoa was a few notches below the Miss, as she saw from the mud trail of brown, grainy sludge that drew a line from the brim to the bottom of the mug. The smoking gun that this was crap instant cocoa. *Oh well, whatevs.* It tasted vaguely like chocolate, and that was good enough for her.

She set down her empty mug.

"Another?" Wendy asked.

"Yes, please."

"Right away, hon." Wendy picked up the mug and turned away.

"Oh excuse me?"

"Uh-huh?"

"Um, I just moved here, and I was wondering, how would I go about getting an apartment? I took a quick look on-line and..."

"Moved here?"

"Yeah."

"Honey, nobody *moves* to Blackstone. Either born here or married in."

Katherine didn't know whether Wendy was insinuating that she'd mistakenly married into it. "Well, I moved here."

Wendy stared at her as if antennae had just sprouted from her head. "Huh."

Katherine nodded her confirmation.

"Well, I don't know that there *are* apartments—" Wendy cautioned.

"Drew's got a place." A man a few places down from Katherine leaned in. He wore a flannel and a trucker cap.

"He does?" Wendy asked.

"Yeah, inherited it from his old man."

Wendy took a step back, smiled, crossed her arms, and pointed at both the man and Katherine. "Seems my job here is done."

Katherine got up from her seat, walked down to the man, and scooted behind the guy next to him. "'Scuse me," she quickly told the guy she'd slid up against.

The guy grunted.

"So, this Drew..." Katherine said.

"Yeah, it ain't fancy or nothin'," the man said.

"The simpler, the better."

The man laughed. "Oh, this place is chock-full of the simplest of simplicity."

"Seriously, all I need is a bed, shower, stove, and internet access."

"How's your credit?"

"Fine."

The man cracked a smile. "I'm just kiddin'. Drew won't give a crap. Long as you give him a deposit and all that."

"That won't be a problem."

"Okay, well, lemme..." He dug his phone out of his pocket and started typing a text.

She took out her phone.

"Number?" he asked.

She showed him.

"What area code is that?" he asked.

"New York."

"That's across the country!"

"Sure is."

"What brought you all the way out here?"

"The trees."

"Ain't got trees in New York?"

"Not as pretty."

"Well, I sent him your number. He should get back to me soon. How do I get ahold of you?"

She pointed to her number in his text.

"Oh right. 'Course," he said.

"Where you stayin' now, hon?" Wendy asked.

Katherine faced her with a sheepish smile. "Um, I hadn't exactly gotten that far."

"Well, there's a motel right up the road. Ain't much to look at, but the bedbugs don't bite too bad."

AUGUSTINE PIERCE

Katherine smiled. "Sounds perfect." She faced the man in the trucker cap. "So, you and Drew have my number." She looked back at Wendy. "I'll need the check and that motel's address."

"Not exactly a grocery store." Katherine entered the tiny mart that the map had led her to believe was a major chain store.

It had ten aisles with refrigerators and freezers along the back wall. The shelves mostly contained snacks and the refrigerators mostly beer.

Oh well, it'll do for now.

"What's wrong with it?" Dean asked over her earbuds.

"It's..." She paused as she passed by the checkout counter and its occupant, a man in his early twenties with bangs dangling in front of his eyes that were glued to his phone. "Small."

"Like, Trader Joe's small or 7-Eleven small?"

"Smaller."

"Whoa."

"Yeah." She walked down an aisle near the opposite end from the cashier so he couldn't see what she was browsing. "Guy's kinda creepin' me out."

"What guy?"

She whispered, "Cashier guy."

THE HAUNTING OF BLACKSTONE MANSION

Dean chuckled. "Probably harmless, Kitten."

"Oh, ew." She laid her eyes on a stain on the floor that looked like it was at least a few days old.

"What?"

"I dunno, but it's gross."

"So what's for din?"

"Sirloin and garlic mashed potatoes."

"You're hilarious."

"Um..." She scanned the contents of the current aisle. There were chips, more chips, and cookies. "Think I gotta keep going."

"Another store?"

"I don't think there is one. Nope. On to frozen." She walked up to the nearest freezer. Inside, she found to her delight that it contained a decent selection of pizzas. "Oh, here we go."

"Frozen sirloin?"

"No, stupid. Pizza."

"Ah."

"Yeah, not great, but what am I gonna do?"

"Go somewhere else?"

"Dean, it's, like, the only store in Blackstone."

"Seriously? How small *is* this town?"

"Small." She picked out a supreme pizza, then went back into other aisles to grab chips and juice. "All right, hold on. Checking out."

"Roger."

AUGUSTINE PIERCE

She walked up to the cashier and set out her items. He hardly took his eyes away from his phone as he rang her up. She took out her wallet and handed him her card. He pointed to the reader right in front of her. *Seriously, dude? Can't be bothered to scan it yourself?* She ran her card. It beeped.

"Receipt?" The cashier finally lifted his eyes from his phone.

"Thanks."

He gave it to her, she collected her bounty, and left.

"Of course, no microwave," Katherine said into her earbuds as she poked around the tiny motel room. She'd checked in just a few minutes earlier and was sizing up the amenities, a generous word to use to describe what the room had to offer.

There was a twin bed, which when she saw it, she imagined her feet sticking out of. There was a shower, which had just enough room to turn around in. There was a table, on which sat her frozen large supreme pizza, and at which she would have imagined sitting at and eating said pizza had there been a microwave.

"What motel is this?" he asked.

She sighed, not exactly in the mood to be teased. "I think it just says Motel on the sign."

"Not even a Motel 6?"

"Not even a three."

"Oh, Kitten."

"Yeah."

"Wait, if there's no microwave, um, how are you gonna eat your pizza?"

"I plead the Fifth."

"No."

"Yeah."

"Do you at least have a fork?"

She chuckled to herself. "Don't hate me."

"I hate you so much."

Katherine sat at the table before her sad, gigantic, frozen supreme pizza. She attempted to make the most of it. "I've had frozen pizza before."

"No, you've had refrigerated pizza, and that was after it'd already been cooked."

She stared at the pizza one more second, silently deciding that she was going to eat it since she'd already bought it and was pretty hungry, but she was at least going to let it thaw. *I'm not a barbarian.*

She stood and crossed to the window that looked out onto the six-spot parking lot.

"What are you doing now?" he asked.

"Just checkin' out the view."

"What's it of?"

She slid the curtains aside. "Trees."

"Lemme see?"

"You wanna see trees?"

"Yeah!"

"Look outside your place."

"Aw, come on."

"Fine." She turned on video and showed him the view through the window. "There. Happy?"

Outside, the parking lot bumped up next to the highway, which ran alongside a black wall of leafy, swaying branches. The sight was mesmerizing. It looked like the forest was breathing.

"Wow," he said.

"Right?"

"Spooky."

"Just a bunch of trees swaying in the breeze."

"Yeah, but still. What's beyond the trees?"

"More trees?"

He laughed. "You're no fun."

Her phone buzzed with an incoming call. "D?"

"Yeah?"

"Someone's calling."

"Who?"

"You don't have to sound *so* surprised."

"Sorry."

"I dunno. I'm gonna jump."

"'Kay-'kay. Night, Kitten."

"Night."

She answered the incoming call and tried not to sound too suspicious. "Hello?" She failed.

"Hello," a deep, rough voice answered. "This Kathy?"

Katherine winced. Not even her own mother ever called her Kathy. "Katherine or... Kat's fine."

"I gotcha. Good evening, Katherine. This is Drew. Carl told me you'd inquired about my place."

"Yeah. Absolutely."

"Well, it ain't fancy."

"Carl warned me. All I need's a bed, shower, stove, internet."

"Uh-huh. Internet's a little spotty."

"Okay?" She wasn't exactly in a place to be picky, but she really did need internet access.

"But it's got everything else you need."

"Good." She noticed he'd completely dropped the question of internet access. She'd have to follow up or figure something else out.

"Look, I ain't a landlord or nothin'. I mean, I guess I technically will be to you, but it's not, ya know, my thing."

"Right." She tried not to sound suspicious, and failed at that too. *Guessing we're getting around to price.*

"How's five hundred a month sound? Not including utilities?"

AUGUSTINE PIERCE

She couldn't believe her ears. She hadn't had a place that cheap since undergrad. "Uh, great. Think I can do that."

"Great. How's your credit?"

"Fine. I mean—"

"Eh, you know what? I don't wanna mess with that. How long you plan on staying?"

"Um..."

"At least six months?"

"Easily."

"Let's say five hundred deposit, first month's rent, six-month lease, call it good?"

"Sounds great. When do I get to see the place?"

"Oh my God. I'm sorry. I completely forgot about that. Like I said, not a landlord."

She smiled. "Clearly." She'd meant it humorously, but he was silent for a second.

"What you doin' tomorrow?"

"I am free."

"I'll text you my office address. Drop by, say, 11:30? We can take care of this before my lunch."

"Sure. Sounds great. Thanks, Drew."

"No problem, Kat. I'll see you tomorrow."

"Great. Talk to you then. Good night."

"'Night." He hung up.

Katherine's phone immediately *dinged* with a new text.

521 E 3rd

THE HAUNTING OF BLACKSTONE MANSION

"All right," she informed the room.

She reached out to close the window's curtains, taking one little moment to gaze again at those trees Dean had called spooky, and entertained the thought that Bigfoot or aliens or some serial killer were watching her from within them. A brief shiver ran up her spine. She chuckled to herself and closed the curtains.

She plugged in her phone near the TV and sat at the table before her pizza. "Well, looks like it's just you and me." She tore into the plastic wrap, took a quick whiff, nodded her approval, and sank her teeth into the first bite. *Ah, frozen pizza.*

3

The next day, Katherine got up bright and early so she'd have plenty of time to drive into Blackstone's downtown, get cash from an ATM, drive over to Drew's address, and take care of rent, with plenty of time to spare between each stop.

That was the practical justification. The truth was she wanted to get up early. She wanted to feel the crisp morning air. She wanted to feel the cold. She wanted to feel uncomfortable. She was even hoping that on getting out of the rental each time, she'd have to jump up and down in place to keep warm.

She exited her motel room, got in her rental, and set out toward Blackstone. On arriving to the downtown area, she searched her phone for the nearest ATM. Luckily, there was one located on the far side of the town square, the opposite end from where she'd parked the day before.

She hurried to the ATM and took care of business. Finishing her transaction, she shoved the bills into her purse. Heading back to the car, she happened to catch a glimpse of the mountain. It was just as tall and majestic as the previous day, though with its shape looming over the tiny ATM machine, it felt almost threatening, like a giant ready to stomp her under its foot.

Her eyes lingered on the dark forested area beyond and above Blackstone. She thought a little about Dean's previous night's observation. *Spooky trees.* It wasn't lost on her that were she to wander up out of Blackstone, it wouldn't be long before she could get completely lost. So all that truly separated her from a dark, forest-y, frozen death was a handful of streets.

A particularly biting breeze reminded her that she was outside and no longer wanted to be. She ran the few feet to the rental and jumped in. She checked the time. Eight forty-five. "Seriously?" She had *hours* left till she was due at Drew's. "Guess I can get a coffee. Or two."

She drove around the square, then up and down some of its surrounding streets. "Not even a Starbucks?" With a shrug, she resolved to return to the diner from yesterday.

The bell rang as Katherine entered. She spotted Wendy immediately and waved.

AUGUSTINE PIERCE

"'Mornin', hon. How was your stay?" Wendy asked.

Katherine shrugged, but tried to sound more enthusiastic. "Good." Though Wendy had been disparaging of the motel, Katherine didn't want to crap all over anything in Blackstone. After all, given the town's size, it was likely everybody knew everybody else.

"What can I get ya?" Wendy asked.

"Um, just coffee. Black's fine. I've got a little wait." Katherine sat at the very end of the counter's right side.

Wendy crossed to Katherine's seat. "Word has it you're gonna rent Drew's place."

"Word gets around."

"Word does."

"Yeah, we'll see if it works out."

"Lemme get you that coffee."

"Thanks." Katherine took out her phone. It still wasn't even nine, and according to her map, it'd take a whopping five minutes to drive over to the address Drew had given her. That meant she had over two hours to blow on, well, she had no idea.

She looked over the map of Blackstone's downtown. There were a few spots of interest. At least one bookstore. One library. An historical society. An elementary school. She did some rough math in her head and figured it'd take at most two minutes to drive around the entire downtown area. And that was being generous.

She sighed, discouraged. She knew full well that Blackstone was small; that was the chief reason she'd picked it, and she was okay with that in most ways. She didn't want to party. She didn't want to go clubbing. She just wanted peace and quiet. But she realized the assumptions that she'd made about her new life here were all based *after* having settled in. All the pre-settling-in errands were turning out to be tall peaks of activity among deep valleys of boredom.

"Here ya go, hon." Wendy placed a steaming mug of coffee before her.

"Thanks." Katherine lifted the mug to her lips, but paused. "Hey, Wendy?"

"Uh-huh?"

"Is there anything to do around here?"

Wendy gave her a little bit of side eye, most likely wondering if Katherine were screwing with her. "To do?"

"Yeah, just somethin' to check out. Local claim to fame?"

"Blackstone ain't exactly Orlando." Wendy now started to sound genuinely irritated.

"No, no. I understand that. I just mean, you know, the local culture. Oldest building, tallest tree, whatever. I've got some time to kill, and I'm not picky."

AUGUSTINE PIERCE

Wendy laughed. In it Katherine could hear more than a hint of bitterness. "Local culture?" She walked back to Katherine's corner of the counter and leaned over, resting her head in her hands. "How long you plan on stayin', hon?"

"I don't know," Katherine answered bluntly.

"Well, the longer you stay, the more you'll learn that if there's one thing that Blackstone don't have, that's culture." She stood up straight, turned around, and headed to the kitchen.

What just happened? Did I insult her? Maybe she thought I was mocking her, the town. Damn it, Kat. When you pay the bill, apologize.

"There's the house," a man suggested.

Katherine looked up, but didn't see anyone looking back at her. "Excuse me?"

"You said you were looking for local culture?"

Katherine found him sitting in the middle of the counter's opposite side. He waved. He had a round, friendly face and wore a Beavers cap. As Katherine recalled, the Beavers were one of Oregon's local teams. She didn't recall from which city or for what sport.

"Uh, yeah, that's right," Katherine said. "Local culture."

"What house?" Wendy asked.

"*The* house. The old Blackstone place," Mr. Beavers said.

THE HAUNTING OF BLACKSTONE MANSION

"The old *what* place? Named after the town?"

"Actually, I think the town's named after it. Or them. The family that built it."

Wendy slowly shook her head.

"You know, Wendy," Mr. Beavers said. "The one up the hill. Where Halloween night we all dared each other to run up and ring the doorbell."

"I never run up to no doorbell," a middle-aged woman, wearing a ponytail, said.

"Well, *we* did." Mr. Beavers nodded at Katherine. "Blackstones were the family that built... well, Blackstone."

"They didn't *build* Blackstone," Ms. Ponytail said.

"You know what I mean." Mr. Beavers informed Katherine. "Old lumber family from back East. One of the richest in the state—in the country—at the time. They *basically* built Blackstone. Had a house up the hill. More mansion. Big ol', creepy, dark-ass place. Folks used to say it's haunted. Hence the Halloween doorbell."

"Haunted?" Wendy laughed out loud.

"Haunted?" Katherine whispered to herself.

Wendy smiled wide at Katherine. "Well, hell, honey, there's your local culture!"

A haunted house? That means old. That means... "How would I get up there?"

"Oh that's easy," Mr. Beavers said. "Take Main all the way down to Nineteenth, take a left towards the mountain—or was it right?—whichever. You're goin' toward the mountain. Keep goin' till Nineteenth turns into Promontory Drive. Your mansion's at the end."

"Does anyone still live there?"

"Oh God, no, not since seventy-two."

"No, sixty-four," Ms. Ponytail said.

"You sure?"

"It was 1964 the last time anybody heard anything outta the Blackstone place."

"I thought it was fifty-one," a man with long white hair suggested.

Hardly able to contain her excitement, Katherine dug a bill from out of her pocket and slapped it down on the counter. "Wendy? This good for the coffee?"

"Yeah, that's fine, but—" Wendy said.

"Sorry about earlier. Wasn't mocking. Gotta go." And with that, Katherine ran out.

"Hey, you don't want your coffee? Or change?"

Katherine dove into her rental so eagerly that she practically fell over onto the gear-shift. She closed the door, not wanting it to even be possible for any townsfolk to hear her. "Oh my God! This is great! A haunted frickin' house? If no one lives there—gotta trace the chain of title—but that's stuff to sell! If it's decent stuff, man, I could set myself up for a while!"

She strapped herself in, fired up the car, and almost slammed the gas, but then remembered the existence of traffic laws. She eased out of her spot and continued down the road as fast as she could legally go.

She followed Mr. Beavers's directions. She'd soon be at Nineteenth. She'd long since left the downtown area and could see dark forest only a few blocks away. *This place is so small!* She reminded herself that this was exactly what Dean had warned her about, but to be cruising through it so quickly was another thing.

She came to the corner of Main and Nineteenth. She looked left. There was the mountain. *Dude was right the first time.* She turned and headed up the hill. As Mr. Beavers promised, it was a straight shot. After a few minutes, and some twisting and turning among the trees, Nineteenth turned into Promontory Drive.

At this point, she was clearly far out of the Blackstone city limits, or so it felt, considering she wasn't even completely sure that it was recognized as an actual city. The main clusters of buildings, the ones surrounding the square, were far below and behind.

AUGUSTINE PIERCE

Strangely, the road ahead looked much darker than she expected. Almost like twilight. She checked her phone's time just to make sure she hadn't entered some magic time-travel portal after Nineteenth had turned into Promontory. *Nope. Only 8:53. Maybe it's the trees.* It was true that the forest had enveloped her and the little road she was following, though that hardly seemed enough to make the whole day feel like it was fading away.

She instinctively turned on her headlights, and, after another few minutes, she came upon a six-foot wall built with bricks so dark they appeared black. "Is this, like, a running theme? Did the family style *everything* as a black stone?" Such a thing seemed way too-on-the-nose, but then it was, of course, possible.

Her headlights streaked across a gate. It, too, was dark, possibly iron. Its frame bore a giant B above twin doors, most likely for Blackstone. She pulled over to the side of the road and shut off the car. She grabbed her phone and got out.

"Damn it!" That cold stung. It felt at least ten degrees lower here than it had in town. "Well, can't be up here too long anyway."

She approached the gate. A giant, chunky lock hung from a chain woven among several bars of its twin doors. She walked right up to the bars and peered up the hill.

THE HAUNTING OF BLACKSTONE MANSION

A road paved in cobblestones so dark they looked like lumps of coal led to the mansion. The road switched back several times until it ended in a loop right in front, most likely first designed for carriages.

The mansion looked at once like the lair of some reject evil wizard out of *Harry Potter* and the warmest, most welcoming abode Katherine could possibly have imagined. It was a colossal, four-story onyx fortress whose trident of conical-roofed towers thrust into the sky with such striking contrast against the overcast gray that it looked as if the building were about to rise up and slay the very mountain it sat upon.

"Kinda verbose." In her limited experience with architecture, it was always the nouveau riche who designed their homes to be so, well, ostentatious. "But looks like it's gotta have, what, two dozen or more rooms? That means assloads of antiques."

She stood back from the gate and looked it over again. "Gonna have to..." She walked over to the wall left of the gate and sized it up. "Man, if grade-school kids can do this..." She felt for the bricks' edges. Decades of weather had worn away some of the mortar, but any grip would be minimal.

She backed away, looked over the wall again to see if she could spy maybe places where bricks had fallen out or any other obvious hand-holds.

AUGUSTINE PIERCE

Nothing.

She retreated to the rental, got in, and fired it up. She scooted it closer to the wall. She shut it off, got out, went to the trunk, and climbed up. From the car's hood, the wall was about chest high to her. While still a little difficult, she was able to climb right over.

The second her feet landed on the cobblestone road, she felt a strange sense of power. It was as if she were arriving on the red carpet to her movie premiere or the lawn of the White House on the first day of her administration. "Is this how rich people feel *all* the time?" She smiled at her silly reaction.

The journey up the road felt like it took much longer than it first seemed it would. She didn't mind, though. As she walked, she admired the surrounding wilderness. "Not bad, Mr. Blackstone, whoever you were."

Nearing the mansion, she noticed far more detail. The walls seemed to be primarily composed of black granite, with dark timbers embellishing its lines between floors and rooms. It boasted ornately sculpted, obsidian Greek capitals and cherubs at all of the corners of its walls and windows. It also displayed a blend of Victorian and Craftsman features from its deep gable roofs to its four tapered pillars that supported the front porch roof at the base of its middle entry tower.

THE HAUNTING OF BLACKSTONE MANSION

In another minute, she reached the carriage loop. She climbed the porch steps with a newly acquired sense of reverence. While she knew nothing about the Blackstones, not even of their existence until less than an hour ago, she felt that such a lovingly crafted home, even if on the verbose side, deserved a certain respect.

Funny, then, that she fully intended to strip it of its valuables to make a boatload of cash. Then again, anyone who would have been offended by such an intention was long, long dead.

She stopped at the enormous oak twin front doors. "Crap." This whole time, driving over, walking up, and now about to place her hand on the honey-colored brass doorknob, it had never crossed her mind that she had no clue whether the mansion was locked. If it was, was she truly willing to break in? She didn't know the building's current legal status. For all she knew, she was technically trespassing right now. Luckily, there were no modern camera systems around to record her terrible crime and no witnesses to see it, so she could always just lie and claim she merely admired the house from outside the gate, but actually smashing a window? That'd be a tougher sell.

She turned the doorknob. Locked. "Ah, come on!" She stepped back a few feet and attempted to size the place up, but found she had to tilt her head all the way back to take in the entire structure. She lowered her gaze and stared at that doorknob.

She looked around as if she were about to find leering witnesses.

No one was there.

She dug around in her purse. "Come on, come on." Tissues, lipstick, and a half pack of gum she'd completely forgotten about. "Come on." She removed the items and held them in one hand while she continued her search with the other. "Wait." She saw the tiny glint of metal. "Yes!" She took out three paper clips.

After replacing the other items back into her purse, she got to work bending two of the clips into makeshift picks. She crouched before the door's lock and got to work.

After a minute of poking around, she heard a *click*. "Right on!" She pulled the sleeve of her jacket over her hand, grabbed the doorknob, twisted it triumphantly, and pushed the door open. It creaked with the low groan from decades of disuse. Inside, she saw a cavernous entryway hall.

With a satisfied exhale, she entered the mansion.

4

The mansion's interior palette was a little warmer and livelier than outside, with chocolate browns and highlights of brick reds and sunflower yellows.

Katherine closed the door. Even though she knew it was highly unlikely anyone would catch her snooping around, she still felt the need to make her presence less obvious.

Her eyes struggled to adjust to the dark. Even with the mansion's large windows, the cover of the surrounding forest filtered out most of the daylight.

She sniffed. A light scent of mildew hung in the air.

Movement. It came from her right.

Great. Someone's in here. A drifter? Bored teenagers? Perfect that I get murdered in some dark and dusty mansion my second day in Blackstone. She whipped out her phone and, unlocking it, saw she had no signal. "Wonderful. Hope I don't need it out here." She tapped on the flashlight and aimed it. The thick beam swam through seemingly endless clouds of swirling dust. "Hello?"

No one answered.

"That all I thought I saw? Dust clouds?" She lifted the beam till it landed on a wall. Starting there, she slowly scanned the room, hoping for interesting details to pop out.

The area was enormous, a grand entryway into the house. She took very slow steps, easing herself into the space. Across from her, at the other end of the room, her light found a grand staircase that rose dramatically back and bifurcated into two separate staircases at the second floor. Twin statues sculpted in black marble stood atop pedestals wrapped in the curled bottom ends of the staircase's railings. They each had a bow and quiver with an arrow knocked and aimed at the other. Cobwebs covered the statues. The most prominent ones stretched from their arms to their feet. Smaller ones reached from their bows' upper limbs, across the arrows, to the ends of the lower limbs.

"Artemis and Apollo."

The statues were carved in such a vibrant, animated fashion that she almost expected them to leap off their perches and fight. She instinctively lowered the light to make sure their feet were still firmly planted.

She lifted her light back to the head of the right statue, Apollo. His marble face was so pleasant, she half expected him to invite her farther into the house, on up the stairs.

"You look like you're original. God, are you two custom jobs?"

She scanned both sides of the staircase. She found twin doors which she hoped opened to dozens of rooms packed with furniture, books, instruments, prodigious metal floor globes, and any number of other fantastic items the Blackstones had gathered over the decades.

She walked up to Artemis. "I'm guessing each of you'd be in the thousands, maybe millions." She threw a glance at Apollo. "If I could pawn you together... Man."

She headed to the door at the right of the staircase. She felt a distinct chill from her right, as if someone had just opened a walk-in freezer. She stopped and scanned. There was nothing but dancing dust particles. She continued on to the door.

It opened with an echoing creak into a hallway that led to the right at a hard angle. She double-checked the angle between the entryway and the hallway. She was no engineer, not even strong in basic math, but it looked really strange. "Is that forty-five degrees?"

AUGUSTINE PIERCE

There were two doors to her left and a blank wall to her right. Past the second door, this hallway met another one, that ran west-east, also at a hard angle to this current hallway, though what actual degrees, she had no idea. "Huh. Gonna have to check that out later."

She closed the entryway door behind her and opened the first door. Another whining creak. "Wonder if I'll ever get used to that." Inside was a cozy room with bookshelves built into the walls, plenty of fancy chairs and tables, and a fireplace. Cobwebs hung from every corner. The stench of mildew was much stronger. "Or that." She nodded at the pieces before her. "Some kind of drawing room?"

She noticed she was standing next to a large leather chair. She examined it closely with her light. "You look like Loscudo leather, probably 1915. A comfy purchase. A piece someone buys who knows what they want. You're definitely not the first and unless the Blackstone fortune took a steep dive after they got you, you weren't the last."

She crossed to the nearest bookshelf, being careful not to bump into or nick any of the probably priceless furniture. Books were tough. Unless it was a first edition of *The Adventures of Huckleberry Finn* or *On the Origin of Species*, the collector had to be a real geek for the genre or author. She could sometimes talk up the volume in question, make the potential customer feel as if they'd miss out if they didn't snap it up, but usually, book lovers knew almost as much as she did, and knew what they wanted.

She lifted her phone's flashlight to eye level to scan some titles. She lightly brushed some cobwebs out of the way. "*Frankenstein; or The Modern Prometheus*, *De Mysteriis Vitae*." She translated. "*On the Mysteries of Life*? I mean, maybe for the right collector. *Frank* could fetch a few."

She exited to the hallway and closed the door behind her. "So surprised no one's ever tried to cash in on this stuff. There must be *some* living relative."

She entered the next room. It also had chairs and tables, and a fireplace, though lacked the built-in bookshelves. It did boast a very nice piano.

"Hello. That looks like a Steinman original." She walked right up to it and examined its curves, lines, and finish. "Whoa. That's a friggin' harpsichord. I didn't even know Steinman made these." She walked around to the instrument's keyboard. Sure enough, there lay the distinctive rosewood and ivory keys. "Damn. You might just be another custom job."

She looked up and pointed her light at various places around the room. Other chairs, more books, a lamp. None of it cheap. All of it tasteful. She nodded, impressed. "I see you, Blackstones. Looks like

I owe you an apology for my earlier supercilious nose, uh, look-down."

She left the room and continued to the oddly angled intersection with the west-east hallway. She looked west and found not only plenty more doors on both sides, but also that this corridor was almost double the width of the one she was standing in. To the east, the hallway ended a few yards away at a curved wall with its own twin doors. "Must be the east tower." She picked the first door nearest the corner to the east. "Good as any other."

Inside, she found she was now standing in a room very similar to the music room, with its own sets of leather chairs, sofas, tables, a few built-in bookshelves, and a fireplace. On many of the tables lay black marble ashtrays. "Huh. The smoking room?"

As if in answer to her question, her light next found a desk near the wall opposite the fireplace, and on it, she spotted a large humidor. She crossed to the desk. "What is it with rich men and cigars?" She pulled her sleeve over her hand and gently lifted the humidor's top. She took a whiff. "Hm. Faint, but pleasant."

She entered the hallway and, in the darkness and angles, found that she already felt disoriented. "I came in"—she shone her phone's light around in a semicircle—"there?" She realized that all she had to do was reverse where she was standing to figure out where she'd stood. "Yeah. There."

She turned to her right, now facing west. This end of the hallway stretched out far beyond her flashlight's beam. She ventured down several yards. Her beam tickled the rounded point of what looked to be the beginning of another black marble sculpture.

Movement. This time from her left.

She jolted her flashlight's beam into the area where she thought she'd seen something, but found nothing. "Hello?"

No one answered.

"Anybody there?"

She still heard nothing. *If it is bored teenagers, they're being awfully quiet.* She stood there a second, tracing the walls and floor as far as her beam reached, but saw no sign of any further movement.

She decided to continue on and soon reached the sculpture. It turned out to be the bust of some middle-aged man, maybe Mr. Blackstone, set back into a wall niche from where he looked to be guarding the center of the house, assuming this was the center. It was covered in dust and cobwebs.

His hair was brushed back in what she imagined was a simple style for extremely wealthy men of the time. It looked respectable and professional without having to look fashionable.

AUGUSTINE PIERCE

He had a wide brow that swooped down over deep eye sockets. His eyes were large and open wide, which she guessed was the sculptor's interpretation of how he usually looked. She liked to think that he had been a curious man.

His nose was narrow and long. It was so prominent, in fact, that it reminded her of the stylized pointy nose of the Wicked Witch of the West from *The Wizard of Oz*. A thread dangled from the tip. Katherine followed it with her light and yelped when she found a spider climbing up. "Ew."

Mr. Blackstone's lips were set in a flat line. Katherine guessed that if he had ever smiled, it wasn't that often.

His chin was sharply defined. So much so that it almost formed a crescent along with his nose. The spider's thread ended there. The crescent was another reminder of stereotypical witch imagery she'd seen since childhood Halloweens.

She was disappointed to find that there was no name etched into the bust or any metal nameplate. She guessed that this was probably due to the fact that in the Blackstone family, his face and name were probably very familiar.

Stepping back from Mr. Blackstone's bust, she scanned the wall on his side of the hallway. She picked a door at random several doors away from her to her right. She opened it to find a fully decked-out kitchen with a black-and-white flat range stove, central island, and cupboards and shelves packed with all manner of fancy tools and utensils.

She wandered in, narrowly avoiding the island. She imagined that in its heyday, this kitchen was likely filled with a private chef, sous-chefs, cooks, and servers preparing and dishing out incredible meals.

She examined a block of cooking knives. "Probably couldn't get much for these." She moved on to one of the cupboards. Inside lay a pristine set of china. "The pride of Mrs. Blackstone? Could be a ton. Gonna have to check the mark."

She walked around the corner, where she found a closet or some other storage space. "Probably just the broom." She opened the door slowly. The closet was empty except for a drawer at the bottom. She slid it open.

Inside sat a bronze cake stand. "Shouldn't this be with the other dishes?" She wrapped her sleeve around the base, lifted the stand up out of the drawer, slid the drawer closed, and shut the closet door. She held the stand up higher so she could closely examine its details with her flashlight.

The base was decorated with sunflowers and roses whose arrangement encircled the initials E+R. "Huh. Strong, distinct molding. Who are E and R?

If famous Blackstones, some collector might pay a fortune for this."

She felt the faintest hint of cold seep through the cloth of her sleeve. It felt as if she were gripping an ice cube with mitten-wrapped fingers. The sensation increased. Soon, it felt like she'd just smashed her fist through the surface of a frozen lake. "Oh my God, that's—"

The stand's base was suddenly so cold it burned. "Ow!" She instinctively tossed the stand across the room. It hit the floor with a loud, echoing *clang*.

She hiked her sleeve back up her arm and rubbed her hands together to warm the fingers that had held the base. "What the hell?" Against her warm hand, her chilled fingers felt like they'd been buried in snow for several minutes. "It wasn't *that* cold in that little drawer, was it?" She shot an annoyed look at the slender closet. "Damn." She sucked on her stinging fingers. They were finally starting to thaw.

She walked over to approximately where she thought she'd seen the cake stand land. She shone her phone's light all around, but didn't see it anywhere. "Great. How am I gonna explain a misplaced cake stand?"

Bang! It sounded like metal smacking against wood. She swung around with her light. "Hello?"

No one answered.

"Okay, seriously, who's there?"

THE HAUNTING OF BLACKSTONE MANSION

She saw no one at all. She sighed. The kitchen suddenly seemed a lot darker, and she felt a lot more alone than she had when she'd first stepped into the mansion.

She shone her light around the kitchen a little more, just to make sure there was no one there. "Should probably get going anyway—"

She froze.

"Wait a minute." Her light was pointed at the kitchen's island. She slowly turned to the left, toward the closet. Her light found the block of knives, the cupboards with the china...

The closet was open.

Her jaw dropped, but she didn't say a word. *What the hell?* Keeping her light trained on the open closet, she backed up awkwardly toward the island and bumped up against it so hard she thought she might accidentally flip backward over it. She slid against it, past it, and retreated to the kitchen door.

She exited into the hallway without bothering to close the kitchen door or even look behind. *Screw it. I'm outta here.* She turned to her right, to the west, and quickly walked several feet before she remembered that she'd entered this hallway from the other direction. She turned around, terrified that she might bump into one of those alleged teenagers. Or worse, a rat. *Rats can't pick up cake stands.*

AUGUSTINE PIERCE

As she sped down the hallway to the connecting one that led out to the entryway, her fear spiraled. *Maybe it's not quiet, bored teenagers. Maybe it's squatters? A serial killer?* If so, why hadn't they said anything when she'd called out?

She opened the entryway door without bothering to cover her hand when she grabbed the doorknob. *Screw it. I'll tell the family I snuck in and touched everything 'cause I-I dunno.*

Whereas before she'd found Artemis and Apollo so intriguing, so inviting, so beautiful, now she only found them creepy. She couldn't even look in their direction for fear that they'd both turn to her and cackle.

She could not reach the front doors fast enough. Crossing the floor of the stupidly big entryway felt like running down the length of a football field. *Was it this huge when I came in?*

Finally, she reached the front doors, wrapped her fingers around a knob, twisted it, jerked the door open, and fled outside.

The cold surrounded her and hungrily nipped at her fingers, ears, and nose. She also noticed something that she'd somehow missed upon arriving at the property. "No birds." She listened just to be sure. The woods were silent. "Weird."

After having been in the dark so long, she'd also completely forgotten that it was still morning. "Crap! My meeting with Drew!" She checked the time on her phone. Eleven twenty. "Great. I'm gonna be late."

She ran down the front steps and the road as fast as she could. Thankfully, since it was all downhill, it didn't take that long.

She saw the gate come up and remembered how she got in. "Crap! My stupid car's on the other side! Nothing to climb on! How am I gonna get outta here?"

Arriving at the gate, she scanned the walls on either side. She saw no more possible hand-holds on this side than she had on the other. Panic again started to gnaw at her gut, at least because she was definitely going to be late for her meeting with Drew, but also because she feared she might truly be trapped on these grounds.

She rubbed her temples. "Think, Kat." She paced in a circle. "If a bunch of snot-nosed brats could get back over in the dark, then there must be a way." She eyed the lock on the gate. "Oh no." As soon as she expressed her dismay out loud, she knew that was her only choice.

She had to climb over the gate.

She walked up next to it and wrapped her fingers around its bars. She wasn't sure why she did this, possibly to test their strength. While she knew little about metallurgy, she suspected that it was possible the bars might crumble and collapse. As she shook them, she was relieved that they held sturdy.

She looked down at the lock and its chain. The lock hung only at about her waist level, so even if she maintained a foot-hold, she still had a ways to go before she could scale the rest of the gate. She clung to the bars and started her first attempt to basically walk up the gate, keeping her feet on the lock and its chain.

She learned instantly that climbing ropes in gym class was a long time ago. The first two attempts to ascend ended in her feet slipping back down to the cobblestones. She sighed as she admitted it to herself. "Right, Kat. It's just gonna suck."

She gripped the bars as firmly as she could. She leaned back till her arms were almost completely outstretched. She kicked her right foot up in an attempt to plant it on the lock, or at least, on a portion of the chain.

She missed. Her second try, she missed again. On her third, she managed to land her foot on the lock, but then it slipped back down. She groaned in frustration and stepped away.

"Wait a minute." She eyed the edge where the gate met the wall. She walked up to it and repeated what she'd attempted before. She used the nearest bars as leverage and started to walk up the wall's bricks.

THE HAUNTING OF BLACKSTONE MANSION

With the help of her shoes' traction, she was able to gain a better hold. The work was still rough, though, as she felt like she had to maintain a white-knuckle grip on the gate's bars in order to provide enough counter-weight against the wall.

With what felt like a Herculean level of exertion, not to mention what probably sounded like gorilla-level grunting and groaning, she was finally able to ascend the wall.

After about two more minutes, she'd barely managed to reach the top of the gate frame. With a lot of grunt-laden scrambling, she climbed over it and sat, very uncomfortably, on top as if she were mounting the world's thinnest, hardest horse. She peered down the other side, which looked at least thirty thousand feet off the ground. She noticed the rental, which she'd completely forgotten she'd parked right next to the gate. "Why didn't I just park in front?"

She thought briefly of scooting along the top of the gate frame so she could drop down to the car's roof, but the long journey along the frame looked too uncomfortable and precarious.

She bowed her head and sighed. "Fine. Let's do this." She kicked her legs over the gate frame and dropped like one of those coal cobblestones in the road behind her.

She hit the ground with a grunt, fell over on her side, and rolled onto her stomach. "Great. Now I'm all dirty and leafy for the meeting with Drew!" She dusted herself off and immediately got in the rental. She strapped in, slammed the door shut, dug out her phone, and was about to place it in its holder, when...

It lit up and buzzed. A new message.

"Great. Who the hell is that?" She checked the number. She recognized it, but didn't remember from where. She started the car, tapped the voicemail play button, and attempted to turn the car around and get on the road without crashing into the gate or some unseen ditch.

"Hey, Katherine, it's Drew. Listen, my morning's gotten a little hectic, so I'm gonna be a touch late. Say, 11:50, noon, if that's okay. See ya soon."

Katherine checked the time. Eleven thirty-five. "Fantastic," she spat. She gunned it down the hill. "I'm gonna be late!"

5

Katherine drove as fast as she believed the law would allow. Luckily, she saw no cops or state troopers anywhere, but she was still scared she might have to talk her way out of something.

She noticed that just as it had grown darker the closer she'd gotten to the mansion, it was now getting brighter the closer she got to downtown Blackstone.

She kept checking the time, those minutes ticking right along. "Damn it, damn, damn it, come on!" For some reason, the journey back to town seemed like it was taking at least twenty thousand times longer than the trip up the hill.

After another minute or so, she reached the corner of Nineteenth and Main. "Okay, where are you, Drew?" She checked the earlier text he'd sent, entered the address into Google Maps, and the app gave her the route. "Oh come on!" It would be another ten minutes at least. Not only would she be late, she'd be noticeably late.

AUGUSTINE PIERCE

She called the number Drew had provided. It rang once before he picked up.

"Hello?" He sounded very suspicious.

"Hey, Drew, it's Katherine."

"Oh, hey, Katherine."

"Listen, don't worry about being late. I'm gonna be a tad on the late side myself."

"Oh, I'm, uh, I'm already here."

She winced and mouthed, "Damn it!"

"How much longer for you?"

"Um"—she decided to stretch the truth—"five to ten?"

"All right." His tone was polite, but restrained.

"Yeah, I'm sorry. Be right there."

Except she wouldn't. As she drew closer to the destination, which initially looked like it was only a few blocks northwest from the town square, the little dot showing her current location on the map kept sliding around, and the directions slid around with it.

She turned a corner with a tall white church, went down two streets, turned another corner, another, and another, all according to the directions, then she saw the white church again. "Oh, you gotta be kidding!"

She pulled over. She knew she was getting dangerously close to the "ten" of that "five to ten" she'd promised Drew. She took her phone off the dash-

THE HAUNTING OF BLACKSTONE MANSION

board, erased the directions, zoomed out on the map, and input the address again. The map zoomed in to the address—only two blocks away. "What? How did I miss that?"

She put her phone back in its mount, got back on the road, and drove those two blocks.

She ended up in a tiny parking lot with three businesses. A laundromat, Blackstone Insurance Co., and a barber shop.

Blackstone Insurance's office space was pretty small. It had a tiny reception area with two faux-leather chairs and a coffee table with a small collection of magazines. In back, there were three cubicle areas decorated with inspirational posters of...

> SUCCESS: HARD WORK + PERSISTENCE

...and...

> MANIFEST TODAY'S DREAMS
> INTO TOMORROW'S REALITY

A short man with a huge red beard streaked in white stood out front.

She mumbled to herself, "Guessing that's you." She pulled up two spaces next to him, grabbed her phone, and got out.

AUGUSTINE PIERCE

That chilly breeze eagerly greeted her again. She tried not to look too uncomfortable, but was pretty sure her rosy cheeks had betrayed that.

"Good morning, Katherine?" He offered his hand.

"That's me! 'Morning!" She shook hands. He had a very firm grip.

He checked his phone. "Oh I guess noon."

"Eh, morning still feels all right."

"Little trouble finding the place?" he asked with just a hint of irritation.

"Um, yeah, I... Yeah. Google was giving me some guff."

"Google's awfully good at that."

"It sure is."

"So, you wanna check the place out?"

"After you."

"Why don't we walk? It's a beautiful day and it's only a few blocks away."

Katherine desperately did *not* want to walk, but she felt she didn't have much of a choice but to agree, given she'd already arrived late. *Guess I'll hug myself extra tight to keep warm.*

"You gonna be warm enough?"

"Oh yeah, fine." She did her best to insist without sounding comically exaggerating. *Let's just get this over with.*

"Right this way." He pointed southeast.

She nodded and followed.

THE HAUNTING OF BLACKSTONE MANSION

"So, what brings you all the way out here to little Blackstone, Oregon?"

"Change of pace."

"Really?" His tone sounded almost as incredulous as Wendy's had.

"Yeah, I just needed some time to recharge, get centered."

"How'd you pick Blackstone? Most folks don't even know we exist. You got family here?"

"No, no. No, uh, no, I don't have family here." *Or anywhere.*

"You just love mountain life?"

She really wanted him to stop asking. *How about this, dude? I'm paying you for your cubby-hole. I wanted something on the opposite end of the country, as small as possible while still being livable. Oh, and a mountain view doesn't hurt.* "Well, I just wanted a small town, where, uh"—she'd completely run out of material, so she started pulling it straight out of thin air—"everybody knows everybody. You know, a real sense of community."

She thought about what Dean might have said in reaction: *Oh my God, Kitten, what a bunch of cheezeball, Hallmark Channel Christmas movie bull. I think I'm gonna—yeah, I'm definitely gonna spew some nice chunky-chunks!*

"Blackstone definitely has that!" Drew laughed. "Not only do we all know each other, most of us have since we were born."

Phew! He seemed to buy that.

They'd reached the northwest corner of the town square. They strolled along the north side.

"And you said you were staying at least six months?" he asked.

"At least. I'm really not sure, but for now, yeah. I just need to, uh—"

"Recharge." He sounded suspicious again, though asked no further probing questions.

"Right."

They reached the end of the square.

"So it's just down here a couple blocks." He pointed straight ahead.

They walked straight east, toward the mountain. After a few seconds of silence, she felt they probably should be saying something, keeping it friendly, especially since she'd been late, so she tried for something easy. "You said you were born here?"

"Yep! Born and raised."

She resisted asking, *How did you not get so bored you went crazy?* "You must like mountain life, then."

"I love it! Far as I'm concerned, doesn't get better than Blackstone."

She tried not to sound too surprised. "Really?"

"Yeah, I don't like big cities. Too busy, too crowded. Gimme the mountains, the trees, the clean air, the clear sunsets."

Huh. He's starting to convince me. "And, uh, Blackstone Insurance?"

"The old man's company. He passed on recently. I'm senior manager."

"Sorry for your loss."

"Thanks, but he was old, sick. He's actually the reason why I have this space. I already got my own place, and, well, no one around here was looking to rent. Well, until now."

And with that, they'd arrived at a residential corner. Nearby stood a little two-story, cream-colored house with a porch and winding stone path. It frankly wasn't much to look at, but it had plenty of room for one person. And it was nice to know that it was so close to the town square.

"This it?" she asked.

"This is it." He dug the keys out of his pocket.

They walked up to the front door and she waited as he unlocked it.

"Haven't had a chance to clean it since your call," he said.

"That's fine. I'm not picky and got plenty of time to clean."

He opened the door to reveal the kitchenette and living room of a small starter home. The kind of place that usually young, married couples would consider a dream come true. In this case, it definitely looked like an old, single man had been here, as there was no decoration, and only one chair in front of a coffee table and a small TV. That and the ugly brown carpet. *That is gonna have to go, when I get to it.*

He threw her an ashamed little grin.

"It's fine. I can spruce it up," she said.

His face fell. "Oh no, this isn't yours here."

Where the hell am I going? There's only the one house! "It isn't?"

"You're upstairs."

"Oh, okay."

"This here's Dad's."

I thought he was dead, the whole reason we're even talking right now. "Gotcha."

"Yeah, this is where he spent most of his time, and I, I dunno, I feel weird about letting someone else live here."

She was very careful not to sound indelicate. "But upstairs is fine?"

"Oh, he never went up there. Too hard on his knees."

Great. So what does it look like? "I understand."

He practically tiptoed around the edge of the living room to the stairs. She was equally as cautious with her footfalls on that dreadful carpet. *So much for sprucing up.*

He led her upstairs where she found two bedrooms, a bathroom, some closet space, and that looked like about it.

"So?" he asked.

She walked down the hallway a bit. "Uh, yeah, plenty of space for me." She faced him and again tried to be sensitive. "If downstairs is your dad's, should I get a hot plate?"

He looked confused, then horrified. "Hot plate? Oh no! No, no, no. You can use the kitchen. Use it all you want. Just keep it clean, and, you know, don't use anything else."

"Gotcha. So, kitchen's good, but the rest is your dad's."

"That's right. Will that work?"

Of course it won't work, you stupid jerk-ass! What am I, a college freshman? Unfortunately, I kinda need something. "Yeah, that's fine. If I have any questions, I can always text."

"So, the deposit and first month was..."

She walked back to him. "A thousand. Yeah, I've got it right here." She pulled the wad of bills from her pocket. "And the internet?"

His mouth opened, but he didn't immediately answer her. "Yeah, gotta switch it over to your name."

Great. How long is that gonna take? "No problem."

He pocketed the cash and took out the keys. "So you're good for the five hundred a month?"

"Yeah. All right there." She pointed to the cash.

"If you don't mind me asking, where you working?"

"I'm currently between... I'm freelance, but I have plenty in savings."

"Uh-huh."

"Plenty. Certainly for the next six months."

"Well, I gotta get to it." He started heading down the stairs. "Utilities are all good. I'll text the numbers so you can change them over to your name."

She followed him down the stairs and back across the side of the living room. "Great. I appreciate that. So, did you want me to sign anything?"

He chuckled. "I ain't got nothin' fancy. I'll e-mail something in the next few days, but you can go ahead and move in."

"Great."

He stepped outside and faced her. "Say, my wife bakes the most amazing peach cobbler. I'll ask her to whip you up a batch. As a welcome-to-Blackstone gift."

"That'd be very sweet."

"You have yourself a great day, Katherine."

"Please, call me Kat. Thanks, Drew."

"Please, call me Drew."

They both chuckled.

"Don't forget your car," he said.

THE HAUNTING OF BLACKSTONE MANSION

"I'll grab it in a few. First I wanna get the lay of the land."

"All right. Talk soon." He waved as he walked away.

"Thanks. Bye!" she said, then closed the door. *All right, now what?*

Katherine thoroughly checked out every room, cupboard, and closet of her new half home. *Linens, maybe a cheap desk.* She headed out to go and pick things up.

Hitting the town square, she was struck by the beauty of its parklike layout set against the mountain backdrop under the midday sun. *It is awfully pretty here.*

In another minute, she arrived at Blackstone Insurance. As she approached the rental, she caught a quick glimpse of Drew moving between coworkers' desks. He stopped, smiled, and waved. She smiled and waved back.

She jumped in, placed her phone, and searched for local bedding and furniture stores. There were scant results. No furniture stores in Blackstone and only one place that looked like it had sheets. *Guess I'll have to order a desk from Amazon, unless I wanna drive for an hour. Wait, does Amazon even deliver out here?*

AUGUSTINE PIERCE

She drove the few blocks to the one store. Their selection was meager, and the owner was inattentive, so she bought the least-ugly set of sheets and tossed it in the car's back seat, then looked for the nearest rental company franchise. She gawked at the result. "Half an hour?" She sighed. "Well, guess I can listen to a podcast and enjoy the scenery."

She got on her way. The drive turned out to be very pleasant, with, indeed, gorgeous scenery and time for quiet contemplation. *Drop off the car, get a ride back, get groceries, figure out the internet stuff, um, look up the mansion—whose ass I gotta kiss to get in on that.* She was glad to have somewhat of a plan, but it definitely felt empty. Even assuming complete success, convincing the next of kin to let her sell off the mansion's antiques, and even if they made a ton of money, what happened after that? "Hopefully, that'd establish me in the community. An antiques broker who can get stuff done." She'd probably need a storefront at some point. She'd need a few pieces, to give potential customers the impression that she had a thriving business. "But even then, how many people are dealing in antiques out here? Maybe I can base the business here, deal with some of the coastal towns?" She was beginning to see Dean's reasons for doubting her move here. "No. I can make this work. I *will* make this work."

THE HAUNTING OF BLACKSTONE MANSION

She soon saw roads, houses, and other buildings appear. She was entering the town of Creek, where the rental company was located, and it was a much, much bigger town than Blackstone. It was so much bigger that she actually felt a little intimidated by its size. "Maybe I should've moved here. No, no. I wanted peace and quiet."

She turned off the highway onto a side street, continued for several blocks, then turned again onto an even smaller street, and into the rental company's parking lot. She grabbed her phone and jumped out.

She walked into the rental company and greeted the cute young woman in glasses behind the front desk and the very cute young man in back who quietly tapped out a rhythm on his leg as he filed. She handed the keys over to the woman.

"And how did you find everything?" the woman asked.

"Perfect. Thanks."

"There's a drop-off fee."

"I know. That's fine."

"Did you fill the tank?"

"No."

"There's a fee for that as well."

"Yeah. It's fine." Katherine took out her card and handed it over.

The woman ran the card and printed the receipt. "Great. Well, Ms. Norrington, you're all set. Thank you so much for choosing—"

"Oh, I don't live around here. I'm gonna need a ride back."

"No problem. Where do you live?"

"Blackstone."

The woman squinted hard. "Where?"

"It's, like, half an hour down the road that way," the man pointed.

"Huh. I've never heard of it."

He shrugged. "You didn't grow up around here."

"All right, Ms. Norrington, well, we can certainly accommodate you, though there's a nominal—"

"It's fine. I'll pay it." Katherine handed over her card again.

"Thanks." The woman ran the card. As she handed it back, she turned to the man. "Can you...?"

"Yeah, I can take her." He nodded. "Right this way, Ms. Norrington."

"Wait..." Katherine paused as she spotted a brochure near the woman's arm. "You guys also sell cars, right?"

The woman perked up, likely at the possibility of a commission. "We sure do. We have a wide range of models from economy to—"

"I'll take whatever you got on the cheap end that has decent storage."

"Of course. Kirk?"

"As I said." Kirk smiled. "Right this way."

Katherine followed him out into the parking lot. He approached a handsome black sedan.

"All right, this has what you need. Not too many bells or whistles. A to B."

"It's perfect."

"Great. Well, let's go back inside. I'll print up the paperwork, you give me your John Hancock, or rather Katherine Norrington, and this beauty is yours."

"After you."

They went back inside, and Kirk took his place next to the woman as he prepared the forms. "So, you grow up in Blackstone?"

Katherine regarded him quizzically. "No."

"It's like I told Annie; no one's heard of Blackstone unless you're from around here, so I figured…"

"No, I just moved there."

"Moved?" He smiled as if she'd just told him a dad joke.

"Yep."

"Why Blackstone?"

Katherine didn't want to say, *Because my whole life collapsed, I needed to get away, and a one-horse postcard town is exactly what I was looking for*, so she half stole Drew's story. "I inherited some property, figured I'd fix it up."

"To flip?"

"I mean, we'll see. Maybe I'll like it enough and just stay."

"If you need any help, contractors, decorators, that sorta thing"—he reached into his pocket and took out a business card—"I know some guys." He deftly offered his card between two fingers.

> Kirk Whitehead
> *Account Executive*

"Still hawking your little contracting business?" Annie grinned coyly.

Kirk ignored her jab. "Like the captain, but with acne." He smiled wide.

Annie rolled her eyes.

Katherine was definitely into that smile. *Good delivery for a rehearsed line.* She accepted the card and looked both it and him over. *Man, it has been a minute. Maybe I can invite him over under the pretense of assessing the house that isn't mine and offer him a cup of coffee to keep him awake for the drive back. Nah, he's, like, fifteen years my junior. If he blew me off, that'd be real awkward. That, and I don't have any friggin' coffee.*

"BS title," Kirk said.

"Sorry?"

"Account executive. I answer phones, take orders, handle customers. But 'executive' sounds better than 'office monkey.'"

THE HAUNTING OF BLACKSTONE MANSION

"I dunno. Office monkey suits you," Annie said.

Katherine laughed out loud.

"Like that?" Kirk asked.

"I dunno. Just sounded funny," Katherine said.

"So yeah, call me anytime about that flip."

"Flip?"

"Your house. The one you're fixing up?"

"Right. Of course. I will definitely do that." With that, the conversation felt like it had ended, so she looked out the window.

"Ms. Norrington?" Kirk called back her attention.

Katherine faced him. Her eyes met his. She felt electricity. "Yeah?"

"If you could just sign here."

"And I'll run your card again." Annie sounded like she was really trying to stay in the conversation.

"Right." Katherine signed and handed Annie her card.

"Well, Ms. Norrington, it was a pleasure." Kirk gave Katherine just the hint of a smile.

She guessed that this was one of his moves. "Pleasure was all mine."

"Seriously, you need help with the flip, gimme a call. We can chat about it over some hot cocoa."

Annie shook her head.

Oh my God, did he just ask me out? Guess he doesn't mind the massive age gap! Crap, maybe I should've in-

vited him over. Oh, I could drink me a glass of that. She blurted, "I love hot cocoa!"

"Great! It's a date. Have a good night." Kirk handed her the keys.

Katherine held up his card. "I'll call you." Feeling pretty good about herself and how this day was going so far, she smiled wide as she left the office.

She drove home in silence, enjoying the scenery in the fading daylight. When she got to her place, she went straight for the refrigerator and opened the door. It was completely bare. "Come on, Drew. Couldn't spring for some welcome snacks?"

After picking up a few essentials at the little store with the creepy cashier, including the nicest brand of hot cocoa she could find, Starbucks, she returned to the house, went upstairs to the farthest bedroom down the hall, and set up her laptop on the bed with her phone as a hot spot. "Gotta take care of this internet." She texted Drew.

> Can I get those utility numbers?

A half minute later, her phone buzzed. It was a text from Drew.

> One sec

> Thanks.

> By the way you're short

THE HAUNTING OF BLACKSTONE MANSION

She asked out loud, "What?"

> In fact, I'm very tall for a woman. :P

Your deposit and first month, it's short

> $1K, right?

Yeah you gave me 980

She lifted her eyes from her phone. "Nine eighty? Oh, the coffee!"

> Sorry. Forgot I got a coffee. Can I make up the difference next month?

That depends, did you wanna be short your first month?

She sighed.

> Where can I meet you?

Office is fine

> Be there in a few.

She slapped her laptop shut, grabbed her phone, and headed out.

In a minute, she was at the town square's ATM. She took out a hundred just in case. In another minute, she was back at Blackstone Insurance.

"How many times can I possibly visit here today?" she asked herself as she got out of the car.

Drew came right out, wearing a big polite smile. "'Evening!"

"I'm so sorry. I didn't mean to stiff you."

"It's all good, Kat."

She took out a twenty and handed it to him.

"And we're all square. Have a good one." He waved and headed back in.

She got back into her car, drove home, and set up her laptop with the hot spot again. "Now to track down whoever can help me hawk those delicious mansion goodies."

6

Katherine looked up the county's public records site, and sent a request. The site informed her that it would take between a day and a week to get a response. She leaned back from her laptop and looked out the window at the mountain. "A week to burn."

She realized it was dinner-time, went downstairs, and took stock of the refrigerator's options. Of course, she'd bought staples, but not really anything she wanted to have for dinner, much less that she felt like making.

She closed the refrigerator door and sighed at the living room. "This town's gotta have at least one restaurant, right?"

She ran back upstairs, grabbed her phone, and looked up nearby food options. There were more than she expected. A Mexican place, an Irish pub, and a gross-looking Italian place. "Think I just need steak, potatoes, and a beer."

AUGUSTINE PIERCE

She headed out and drove a few blocks to south of the town square. There stood Sean's Irish Pub and Grill. It was a simple establishment with seating outside that she imagined was probably pretty lively in the summer.

Outdoor drinking in the summer. Though she wasn't a heavy drinker herself, she always enjoyed settling outside with Dean, his husband Ryan, and other friends, chatting over a pint or three. She felt suddenly and intensely sad that she likely wouldn't ever do that again.

"I can at least get me a beer." She swallowed the lump in her throat, then got out and went in.

Sean's was noisy and dark, but not overwhelmingly so. She went straight for the bar, and the bartender passed her a menu, with a nod. The menu had a surprising number of options beyond blooming onions and fish and chips. She was feeling boring, though, so decided on the steak and mashed potatoes.

She set down her menu. The bartender came right over.

"Evening, ma'am," he said. "What can we get you?"

"Steak and potatoes. Feeling basic." *Why am I defending myself?*

"Anything to drink with that?"

"I totally forgot about that." She picked up the menu and skimmed the drinks. As with the surprising number of food options, there was a surprisingly large number of craft beer options. One in particular leapt out at her. "I'll have the chocolate stout."

"Comin' right up." He put in the order.

Dean would've made fun of me: "You know it doesn't actually have chocolate in it."

"I know that." I could've called. Nah, too loud in here. Maybe I'll ring him after dinner.

"Doesn't even taste like chocolate."

"Yeah, I've had chocolate stout before."

"Just sayin'."

"Your stout." The bartender placed the pint in front of her.

She took a small sip. It was good. *Tastes a little like chocolate.* She turned around on her stool to survey the place. It was half restaurant, half bar, with about a dozen tables all packed with friends and couples, two pool tables, at which a group of twentysomething friends played, and a small area she imagined was meant for dancing.

She paid a bit more attention to the guys playing pool. None of them was particularly unattractive or really popping on her radar.

Dean's totally gonna tell me, "Should've taken Kirk home."

"Yeah, maybe. Whatever. Shut up."

She turned back around on her stool to face the bar. She ran her eyes up and down the menu, not reading, more studying the shape of the letters, their loops and angles. *I forgot how boring it is to wait for food.*

She set the menu down and resolved to just listen to the music. It didn't feel like too much of that before a plate piled high with delicious-looking food slid before her.

"Bon appétit." The bartender smiled.

"Thanks." She dug in. *Damn!* This was the second time in two days that the food in Blackstone was so good. *What do they put in the water?*

She wolfed down her dinner in only about three minutes. She then sipped on her beer. She wasn't that thirsty, so preferred to savor the almost-but-not-quite chocolate taste.

"Don't think I've seen you around here," a young-sounding voice said with a pinch of too much charm.

Yep, should've taken Kirk home. All right, let's do this. She glanced to her left. A guy in a trucker cap and goatee looked like he was trying to decide between smiling, playing it cool, looking her directly in the eye, and pretending the wall offered something more visually intriguing. *Is this, like, your first time trying to pick up a chick in a bar?* "Yeah, I'm new." She didn't really want to have this conversation, but she didn't want to not have it either.

"Next round's on me. What you havin' there?"

THE HAUNTING OF BLACKSTONE MANSION

"Chocolate stout, but I'm good with this one." He looked the tiniest bit familiar, and she realized that he was from the group of friends at the pool tables. She threw a quick glance back at them. Sure enough, several were looking on to see how he was doing. *Oh boy.*

"Ah, come on. Lemme get your next." He called to the bartender. "Dude, Nick, another choco stout for the lady."

"*Lady*, that's classy," Katherine said.

"Yeah?" Mr. Goatee sounded way too eager for her approval.

She shrugged. "Better than 'ma'am.'" She sipped.

"Oh no"—he chuckled nervously—"you're no ma'am."

"Oh no?" she asked, feigning offense.

"Far too pretty."

She pointed an index finger at him. "There you go."

Nick set the second stout in front of her. "M'lady." He grinned with the wisdom of years and years having witnessed dozens of young men having choked with dozens and dozens of young women.

She rolled her eyes. *No way I'm gonna drink this.*

Mr. Goatee must have noticed the eye roll as his tone shifted into full-on desperate. "So, uh, what brings you to our delightful little burg?"

She faced him and continued sipping. "New start."

"From what?"

"Old life."

"What happened?"

"You don't wanna know."

"Divorce?"

She had to laugh. *Me married?*

"That was funny?" he asked, sounding very hopeful.

"In the worst way."

He called to Nick, "Hey, man, can I get a Bud?"

She guessed he either needed an injection of some liquid courage, a quick distraction to regroup, or both. She gulped down more of her stout, and was relieved to find that she only had about two swallows left.

"So, uh..." Mr. Goatee began, turning back to her.

"What do you know about the mansion outside town?"

He looked delighted that she was asking him something, and something that he probably knew all about. "Blackstone mansion?"

Thought that was obvious. "Yeah."

"Uh, it's this huge place up in the hills, supposed to be haunted."

"Haunted?"

"Yeah."

"You ever been out there?"

THE HAUNTING OF BLACKSTONE MANSION

"Yeah, it's like a rite of passage. Halloween ain't done till you've made the doorbell run."

"So you've rung it?"

"No, I was, uh, keeping watch in case any cops showed up. You know, private property."

"Right. Every year?"

"Huh?"

"You kept watch every year?"

"I only went twice."

"Gotcha. So any truth to the rumors? That it's haunted?"

"I mean, I never saw anything, but some friends, yeah, they said they felt cold spots, saw shadows."

"Shadows?" Maybe he was referring to the movements she'd seen out of the corner of her field of vision.

"Yeah, one friend said... It's gonna sound crazy."

"I like crazy."

"He said he saw a shadow move."

"Shadows move all the time." She pointed to the one her arm cast on the bar as she lifted her beer for a sip.

"No." He became serious. "He said he saw a shadow *in* the shadows. Like, it was its own, I dunno, entity."

She felt a tingle up her spine. *That's what I saw. Or was it?* "Some folks said it was abandoned. That true?"

"Yeah, I dunno when. Nineteen twenties, I think. Legend is, some crazy shit went down and the family just fled."

"As in ran away?"

He nodded. "Never returned. Just left the place to rot."

That would explain what I saw with all the furniture and kitchen stuff. Certainly looked like it'd been abandoned. "Listen..." She paused, suddenly considering she should probably let him down easy because of what she'd seen and heard of so far, Blackstone was small enough that she'd either run into him again or someone who knew him. "What's your name?"

"Bobby."

"Bobby, as you can see, I'm done with my dinner, and"—she downed the last of her stout—"my drink, so I am gonna go back home, curl up with a documentary on the fall of Rome or something, and pass out."

"You sure?"

"Yep." She nodded at Nick. "Can I get the check?"

Nick gave her a thumbs-up and nodded approvingly, most likely agreeing with her decision not to engage Bobby any further.

"You, uh, okay to drive?" Bobby asked.

"Thank you very much for asking, Bobby, and for your concern. It's not far. I'll be fine."

The check arrived. She handed Nick her card.

THE HAUNTING OF BLACKSTONE MANSION

He ran it in a snap, and handed it back. "Thank you so much. You have yourself a good night."

"You too." She offered Bobby a parting nod. "And you as well."

"Oh yeah, uh, thanks." Bobby sounded as if he were calculating exactly where he'd gone wrong. He picked up her would-be second stout and glugged a good half.

She headed out, paused at the door to see how Bobby's friends were reacting—pointing and mocking laughter all around—and left.

She got in her car, sent a text, waited two seconds, and answered her buzzing phone.

"Hey, hey," Dean said over the phone's speaker.

She placed the phone in its mount, started the car, and got on her way. "So I just got hit on."

His voice continued over the car's speakers. "Congratulations. That didn't take long. And how'd our Prince Charming do?"

"Not terrible, but I just, meh."

"Please don't tell me you're turning in your va-gee-gee."

"No, I'm not. And don't ever call it that. My lady part is a beautiful, wonderful flower."

"Of course it is, Kitten."

She passed the town square. "No, I just, I don't wanna slut it up in bars."

"And that would be because...?"

AUGUSTINE PIERCE

"Small town? They all know each other?"

"Fair point. Wouldn't wanna pull a *Grey's Anatomy* pilot."

"What?"

"Sigh. You should've watched with me. The main character, Meredith Grey, she sleeps with this guy who turns out to be her boss."

Katherine laughed as she pulled up to the house. "You either know too much about that show or I know too little."

"Obviously, the latter."

"All right, I'm here. I'll call if I can't sleep."

"'Night, hon."

"'Night."

7

Katherine slept till noon the next day. As soon as she got up, she changed the bed's sheets and put her clothes away. Then she went downstairs and made herself some breakfast. She thought about ringing Dean, but decided she didn't want to bother him on a Sunday, especially considering that most Saturday nights, he and Ryan usually went out and had to spend much of Sunday recovering.

She stared out the front door window as she sipped her hot cocoa. For the first time since arriving in Blackstone, she didn't have anything she needed to do, or at least anything she could do, so she decided that she'd spend the day thoroughly exploring the town. *That should burn at least an hour.* After that, she figured she'd just spend the rest of the day watching documentaries or YouTube videos. *Nothing like a good YouTube rabbit hole. Almost as good as Wikipedia ones.*

Wandering the streets later, she decided to be completely methodical. She'd walk all the way to the southeasternmost corner and work her way northwest one block at a time.

Outside of the downtown core, most of the area was residential. So she spent most of the time attempting to catalog the common features of the houses. Unfortunately, Blackstone boasted little architectural variety. Most homes were one-story ranch houses, the only difference being the style of the paths to their front doors: concrete, brick, or gravel.

Every time she reached the easternmost side, she looked over to the foothills of Mt. Hood and imagined the mansion. Bobby's words had haunted her. Shadows. *Did I see any when I was there?* She wasn't even sure how she'd be able to tell. What did a shadow in a shadow look like?

It took a little under two hours to walk the complete grid. When she reached the northwest corner, she realized that her feet were hurting and by the time she'd get back, they'd be throbbing. Sure enough, when she finally reached the house, all she could think about was a hot bath in which to soak her feet.

She immediately ran upstairs, drew a bath, and marinated. She hadn't realized how tired she was till she came to in a bathtub full of lukewarm water. She got out, dried off, threw on some pajamas, and got into bed to watch YouTube.

THE HAUNTING OF BLACKSTONE MANSION

She passed out again, and when she woke it was already evening. She made herself some dinner, contemplated returning to Sean's, decided she didn't want to risk bumping into Bobby again, so returned to bed and lost herself in a Wikipedia rabbit hole that started with cake stands—inspired by the one she'd found in the mansion—and ended at Clovis I, king of the Franks. It was then that, despite her sleeping in and the bathtub nap, she passed out for the night.

The buzz and chime of her phone immediately woke Katherine up. Lifting her head and opening her eyes, she found that she'd passed out pretty much right on her laptop's keyboard. She swept her fingers across it to check for any signs of drool. She found no wetness. *Thank God.*

She grabbed her phone and sat up to check the message. It was e-mail. The public-records clerk had already written back. She checked the time. It was almost noon. Somehow, now knowing the time, and knowing it was almost midday, made her think of breakfast, which made her hungry. But first, she had to deal with whoever owned the mansion.

She woke her laptop up, jumped on e-mail, skimmed the message, and found the pertinent information. A Mr. Jordan Blackstone, phone number 503-555-1192, resided at 1120 NW 9th, unit 1401, Portland, Oregon. She looked up the address. It was in a modern building called the Vista in a fashionable part of town known as the Pearl District. "Huh. Must be a direct descendant. Kept the name and everything."

She added the number to her list of contacts on her phone. She knew doing so was presumptuous. She hadn't even spoken to the guy, much less convinced him to let her sell off his pile of antiques, but she had a feeling she was going to need this number.

She slapped her laptop closed, jumped out of bed, held up her phone to call, and paced. It had been a very long time since she'd had to establish rapport with someone, even longer since she'd had to make a cold call. She imagined this was what guys had to do to prepare themselves for calling a girl to ask for a date.

She paced back and forth, the length of the bedroom, several times. She kept rehearsing what she was going to say. "Hey, Mr. Blackstone, my name is Katherine Norrington. You don't know me." She winced. "Don't say that. Of course he doesn't know you." Ultimately, she decided ripping off the proverbial bandage was the best thing to do.

She punched in Jordan's number. It rang three times before it was picked up.

THE HAUNTING OF BLACKSTONE MANSION

"Hello?" a curious, but also very skeptical, young male voice asked.

"Hello, Mr. Blackstone?"

"Yeah. Who's this?"

"Hi. I'm Katherine Norrington. I'm an antiques dealer."

"A what?"

"An antiques dealer. I find, assess, and sell antiques."

"Not interested. Thanks."

"No, wait, Mr. Blackstone. I'm not trying to sell you anything. I'm actually trying to make you, well... a lot of money."

"I don't understand."

"According to public records, you're the current owner of the Blackstone mansion."

"Blackstone... Isn't that the dump rotting on that hill by Mt. Hood?"

She didn't love his description, but reluctantly agreed. "Yes."

"Wait, you looked me up?"

She was getting a little nervous. "I had to follow the chain of title in order to find out who currently controlled the estate."

"Slow down, Anita."

"Katherine."

"What?"

"My name. It's Katherine."

His tone was of supreme confidence as if she had truly gotten her own name wrong. "I could've sworn you said Anita."

"No."

"You're saying that you wanna sell the crap that's been sitting in the house?"

"Yes."

"For, like, the last hundred years?"

"Um, yes."

"What's in it for you?"

"A, uh, modest commission."

He chuckled. "I bet."

"I assure you, Mr. Blackstone, I earn it."

"I bet you do. Wait. The house has just been sitting there for, like, decades."

"As far as I know."

"How do you even know what's in it?"

Crap. How would I know? "Um, I took a glance."

"From the road? Isn't the house, like, twenty thousand miles from the gate? I don't remember. Haven't seen it since I was a kid."

"Mr. Blackstone, I do apologize. I'd heard of the house, was curious, so I drove out there simply to check it out, and I sorta took a closer look."

"You trespassed on *my* property?"

Damn it. "Technically, yes." She heard nothing but silence on the other end. "I'm very sorry. I know I shouldn't have. I was only curious, but I... I can make you a lot of money."

He laughed. "Slow your roll, Kathy."

Oh God, don't call me Kathy.

"I'm not gonna call SWAT or anything."

"That's a relief, thank you."

"But I'm not interested."

"Excuse me?"

"I'm good. No interest in selling any antiques."

"To be clear, Mr. Blackstone, you wouldn't have to do anything at all. I'd represent your estate, handle everything, then hand you a check."

"No thanks."

"A very sizable check."

"How do you know how big the check would be?"

"Well, I assume—"

"Assume? You don't know?" He laughed out loud. "Oh, you're hilarious, Kathy. As hard as you're pitching, I thought you would've moved it all out to the front yard, tagged it, and cataloged it by now."

"I saw a few pieces, yes."

"Ah, so you didn't *just* walk around up there?"

"No. Again, I apologize. I was curious."

"So you broke in?"

"I, uh, improvised."

"Listen, Kathy, this has been really entertaining, but I gotta go. You have a good day now."

AUGUSTINE PIERCE

"Mr. Blackstone, please, just give me one second—"

He hung up.

Her phone-holding hand dropped to her side. She exhaled hard. "Great job, Kat. Now what?"

"Wow, he's like a legit playboy." Katherine was reading up on Jordan Blackstone on her laptop while shoveling scrambled, partly burnt eggs into her mouth.

Pictures of Jordan showed that he was very handsome, in his early thirties, his hair often styled with the right amount of muss to make it look like it hadn't been styled. His face was clean and relaxed, his smile easy, his teeth perfectly straight and bright white.

"How so?" Dean asked over the phone.

"He owns the condo in Portland, really nice neighborhood too."

"Kitten, owning a condo in the nice part of town does not a playboy make. Otherwise all up-and-coming gay men would be playboys. Huh, actually..."

"So not only did he inherit the Blackstone family estate as an only child, but looks like he's an—Oh God, you're gonna love this."

"What?"

"He's a DJ."

"Seriously?"

"Goes by DJ JB."

"Wow, that's hard to say."

"And he's an influencer."

"No."

"Yeah. Instagram and everything. But, ooh…"

"What'd you find?"

"A few articles on *Forbes* and *Insider* looks like he's kinda burning through his cash. Several failed start-ups he invested in."

"Sounds like he played his boy a little too hard."

She rolled her eyes at his stupid joke. "God, Dean."

"So what's the plan?"

"I have no plan."

"That usually works for you."

"Not this time."

"So what are you gonna do?"

"I need to get his attention."

"You could stand outside his window, hold up a boombox, and play some Peter Gabriel."

"He's on the fourteenth floor."

"Hold it extra high."

"I'd need to drive out to see him."

"So, where is he?"

"Northwest Portland."

"Wait, isn't that kinda far?"

"Like, an hour and a half."

"Ah, you can make that. Easy! Bring some pretty piece from the house, blow him away with your skills, and he'll be begging you to sell it and the rest."

"Wow, Dean, that's actually a really good idea."

"See? That's why they call me Dean the Machine."

"Nobody calls you that."

"Uh, Ryan does. All the time. Especially when we're—"

"Whoa, TMI." She giggled. Then she considered his suggestion. "Only problem is…"

"What?"

She sighed. "Nothing. It's just the last time I was up there…"

"Something happen?"

"You'll laugh at me."

"Kitten, did Casper go, 'Boo!'?"

She hesitated. "No. Nothing like that."

"Oh my God, Katherine Norrington, did you see a ghost?" He laughed.

"No, D, it wasn't a sheet with eye holes! It was… Forget it. Told you you'd laugh."

He tried to calm his giggles, failed, took some deep breaths, and finally was able to keep it under control. "I'm sorry, sweetie, but you gotta admit. It does sound funny coming from you. I mean, you didn't scream once when we watched all those *Nightmare on Elm Street* and *Hellraiser* flicks as kids."

"No, this wasn't that. It was probably just a cat or a drifter or something."

"A cat *or* a drifter?"

"I dunno. It was weird."

"How about this? You go out, buy yourself the biggest, bulkiest flashlight you can find, drive your sexy ass out there, ring me up, if I'm not too busy, I might even answer, then I'll go along with you, over the phone, in spirit. Pardon the pun."

"You're a dick." She smiled, then sighed. "Actually, a decent flashlight is a great idea. I could barely see a damn thing in there last time."

"See? Dean the Machine strikes again."

"Stop calling yourself that."

"Never!"

"I'm gonna finish up here, get that flashlight, and ring you back."

"If I'm not too busy."

"You won't be."

"Talk soon."

They hung up. She gobbled the rest of her breakfast, barely cleaned up, threw on some clothes, and ran out the door.

Katherine found a hardware store a block west of the town square. She quickly found a flashlight that looked like it would suit her needs. It was big enough that she could barely hold it in one hand. She also grabbed two sets of batteries, just in case the first set were duds. Assuming she'd want to handle items she'd find, she got a box of rubber gloves. Finally, she located a bolt cutter to take care of the mansion gate's pesky chain.

Jumping in her car, she set the bolt cutter in the back seat, the flashlight, batteries, and gloves on the passenger seat, her phone in its holder, and called Dean.

As the line rang, she pulled away, and started on the journey to the mansion. After what seemed like twenty rings, he finally picked up.

"Ooh, sorry, Kitten, pretty busy right this second."

"Are you serious?" She sounded far more desperate than she intended.

"No, of course not!" He laughed. "So, what are we lookin' at?"

"It's about fifteen minutes up to the mansion, most of that down this country road."

"Fantastic. *Shining* vibes all the way."

"Why'd you have to bring up *The Shining*?"

"Um, because it's relevant."

"After that, there's a gate, then the cobblestone road up to the house."

"Why do you bring that up?"

"Because coverage was spotty last time. I might lose you there."

"Gotcha. Cobblestone road equals dropped call."

"Might equal. Hopefully, we'll last till the actual house. If not, I guess I'm on my own."

"If we do drop, call me as soon as you can once you're done. If I can't be there for you, I can be there after."

"Sounds good." She smiled. By now, Nineteenth had become Promontory, so she was on the home-stretch to the mansion. She updated him as to her whereabouts.

"So when'll I lose you?"

"Probably another five minutes or so." Again, her surroundings felt darker as she delved farther into the woods, closer to the mansion. *Is this seriously a trick of the light? The trees don't seem* that *thick.*

"Did I lose you already?"

"No, no. I just, it's this weird thing. This part of the road, it always feels like twilight, no matter the time of day."

"Maybe it's your mind playing tricks on you."

"Maybe."

"Or maybe it's just the way the trees look."

"I thought of that, but I've been around trees, even thick woods, and it didn't look like this."

"Maybe Oregon trees are different."

"Yeah, Dean." She chuckled mockingly. "Because Oregon trees obey a different set of optics laws than other trees in the country."

"Hey, I'm just sayin'."

She saw the gate. "Almost show-time. See how this goes."

"I'm ready."

She pulled up to a similar spot as she had before, parked, grabbed her flashlight, extra batteries, gloves, and her phone. She put in her earbuds, picked up the bolt cutter, and got out.

"You gone in yet?" he asked.

"No." She shoved the second set of batteries into her jacket pocket. "Not quite." She tested the flashlight on the gate. In daylight, its beam was faint, but it looked solid. She clicked it off. "Okay, here we go."

She walked up to the gate and lifted the bolt cutter to see how much of a pain this was going to be. It looked like the cutter could easily snip into the chain's links. She positioned it and gave it a hefty squeeze.

Snap! The cutter made quick work of the link. She clumsily unraveled the chain and left it and its lock in a pile on the ground. *Someone could've done this years ago*, she rationalized her breaking in. She pressed the right door. It was a little stingy, but soon its hinges whined and it opened. She slipped in. "Dean?"

THE HAUNTING OF BLACKSTONE MANSION

"Still... here..." His voice was already breaking up.

"This may already be over. You're starting to break up."

"Yeah, I'm"—there was a significant pause—"hearing you."

The second she set foot on the cobblestone road, it was like she had set off an *Indiana Jones*-style trap. The line died with that irritating triple beep. "Dean?" she asked futilely.

Nothing.

She sighed heavily. She didn't know which was more frustrating, the call having dropped or that she had actually hoped it would last to the mansion. "Right. Guess it's just you an' me, light." She bobbed it up and down as if it were nodding.

She hiked the rest of the way to the mansion's front doors and paused right before its bottom step. "What am I afraid of? If there's a squatter, I can beat him with the light. Then again, if that happens deep inside, I'll have to use my phone's light to get out." She was hating how flawed this plan was, the fact that it had taken her this long to fully consider that, and the fact that all of this effort might be in vain if she didn't end up convincing Jordan to let her represent the estate.

She sighed again. "Let's just do this." She clicked on the flashlight in anticipation of the heavily dusty darkness, and forged ahead, stomping up those front steps.

8

Opening the mansion's right front door, Katherine was delighted to see that the outside light had drastically dulled her flashlight's beam. It was now strong, bright, and cast a wide circle of light on everything it passed by. Artemis and Apollo, as big as they'd seemed when she'd first encountered them, now appeared dwarfed like small children under stadium lighting.

She felt like she was in control.

"All right. Need a piece I can carry that's worth something, has hopefully a storied history, so I can wow Jordan."

Going to the door on her right had ultimately led to the kitchen where she'd discovered the mysteriously self-freezing cake stand in the broom closet, so she instead chose to go forward, up that enormous staircase.

As she approached the statues, she kept her focus dead ahead, the light a few feet above her, so as not to be caught by surprise by anyone or anything that chose to jump out. "You're being ridiculous, Kat. They're just statues."

Passing by them, she couldn't help a quick look to her left, at the back of Artemis's head. To her intense relief, she found no sign of movement. The statue was not about to turn around and cackle. Despite its lack of movement, though, she chose to go up those steps just a little bit faster.

As she neared the second floor, her light bounced up and down at first only on the steps, then also into the empty dark space beyond the top of the staircase. Reaching the top, she saw that the light shone very brightly on a straight vertical line, then faded along two sides. She realized what she was seeing was the corner of two hallways meeting at a hard angle. "What a weird floor plan. Why build all these hallways based on a geometry lesson?" She caught the shining highlights of an angular pattern. She paused and aimed her light.

The pattern was set in a square metal plaque fixed to the corner, and what looked like about six feet above the floor. It was covered in dust and cobwebs. The main visual thrust of the pattern was an equilateral triangle pointed up. Each point had a little circle attached. From the center of the triangle's right and left sides, two twin lines reached down toward each other, connecting to the bottom side.

THE HAUNTING OF BLACKSTONE MANSION

The twin lines and bottom side together formed a bucket-like shape.

"Huh. Wonder what that is."

The twin hallways had two doors each on the same side as the plaque. The other sides of both hallways were blank. She realized this area was simply one floor above where she'd found the library and drawing room.

She picked the second door on the left side. Approaching it, she heard the floor creak underneath her feet. "God, Kat, chill. It's just you. No one's gonna jump out." *Why am I so jittery? Dean was right. Nothing ever scares me! Why now?*

She opened the door with her bare hand. She figured since the cat was out of the bag with Jordan already knowing she'd trespassed, it made little difference now if she were to leave evidence of it. She also had the impression he wasn't the type to have people arrested for such trivial infractions. She guessed that he'd consider something like that not worth his time.

The room was a salon, looking very much like the drawing room from yesterday. She looked up and down the walls with her light. There were the usual sofas, chairs, and tables. None of the objects her beam touched grabbed her attention. It wasn't that she assumed nothing was valuable in here, but part of her mission was to find the piece around which she could weave a narrative that would grab Jordan's attention. *Gotta be something special. A book's not gonna do it and I can't carry a sofa.*

She closed the door and continued down the hallway till she met the west-east hallway. To her left, she found the entrance to the west tower. She continued past the west-east hallway. There were several doors on each side, but for some reason, she suspected there'd only be more salons or drawing rooms.

This current hallway only lasted a few yards before it met another that shared the dimensions of the west-east corridor. *Down the left must connect to the west tower*, she reasoned. *This floor plan just keeps getting stranger and stranger.* She continued to the right, finding many more doors on both sides.

She arrived at a north tower. The hallway she'd been following met a twin corridor. These two hallways came together at the same angle as the ones at the top of the entryway staircase. The tower had a pair of impressive double doors carved with all kinds of twisting, turning flourishes and a giant B at the center. These doors reminded her of the ones at the mansion's front entrance. "The master?"

As she approached the doors, she again noticed the creaking underneath her feet. She was starting to get used to the sound, but a sense of unease lingered at the back of her head each time she heard it.

THE HAUNTING OF BLACKSTONE MANSION

Reaching the doors, she eagerly gripped the doorknobs, turned them confidently, and flung them open. "Boo-yah!"

As she'd suspected, inside lay an incredible master bedroom decked out in the most opulent finery of its day. Every surface was caked in dust. Cobwebs seemed to reach from every corner to every other one. The floor was covered in what were clearly handwoven rugs in exquisite Islamic geometry, she guessed directly imported from what was then called Persia. The four-poster redwood bed had burgundy silk curtains, which also looked handwoven. The bed was made with cream pillows and linens, lined with hand-stitched Burano lace from Venice, Italy. The vanity was hand carved from walnut. The huge windows were draped in crimson silk curtains. She was tempted to open them to admire what was undoubtedly an unrivaled view of Mt. Hood, but feared that if she even laid a finger on them, they'd disintegrate. The lamp chandelier was the masterpiece, hanging watchful over the room, its brass frame decorated with hundreds of bulbs, fashioned in Murano glass also from Venice. "Wow!"

She let her flashlight dangle as she took out her phone. She snapped a bunch of pictures. Even if she could convince Jordan to auction the items from this room only, the commission alone would set her up for years.

AUGUSTINE PIERCE

Holding her phone in one hand to take more pictures, she gripped her flashlight again. As she greedily stepped farther into the room, hoping to uncover more treasures, her beam fell on Mrs. Blackstone's vanity, onto a particularly nice piece placed up against the mirror.

It was a jewelry box assembled from dark-stained oak with black leather trim. The top was inlaid with Indonesian silver in an intricate pattern of vines and leaves that had been skillfully handcrafted. A tiny key still stuck out from the keyhole in front.

She set her flashlight near the edge of the vanity, pointed at the ceiling. She hovered there a moment, taking in the box's beauty. She took several more pictures. "Mrs. Blackstone's pride and joy." She took out the box of gloves and put on a pair. She carefully turned the key, as if she might break it off in the hole. She slowly lifted the lid with her fingertips. Inside there lay a tray with a set of emerald earrings in the right compartment and a matching set of bracelets in the left. She lifted the tray and set it aside. "Oh my God." At the bottom of the box, she found a stunning emerald-and-diamond necklace, the centerpiece a chunk of ice half the size of her fist.

She lifted the necklace out of the box and held it at arm's length over the flashlight's beam. The gems and diamonds sparkled, tossing little dancing rays of white and green all over the room. She smiled at the delightful sight. "So beautiful."

She paused in her admiration. A tiny, dark shape had appeared at the center of the diamond. "Oh no, is that a blemish?" The shape was a long oval, but otherwise had no discernible detail. She peered closer. She could swear it was actually starting to resemble a fingernail-sized silhouette of a person. As the necklace dangled in her hands, though, the shape slid ever so slightly across the diamond's surface. *It's not a blemish, it's a reflection!*

She shouted and spun around, completely forgetting both the necklace and the flashlight. "Who's there? Who is that?"

Tink! The necklace dropped on top of the flashlight.

Thunk! The flashlight fell off the vanity.

The room plunged into almost complete darkness.

"Hello?" She hoped her voice would sound firm and authoritative, but it instead sounded shaky and meek.

Deep in the shadows that now cast themselves across the floor and furniture, she was sure she saw the source of the reflection in the diamond, a figure in all black turning away, then walking—no, gliding—out of the room. *A shadow in a shadow!*

AUGUSTINE PIERCE

A crippling chill shot straight up her spine. She heard stilted breaths escape her lips. She did not dare show her back to that side of the room for fear that whatever she had just seen leave might come back.

She sank to her knees and awkwardly shuffled over to where the flashlight had fallen. Her fingers fumbled around the handle as she attempted to pick it up. She was finally able to grip the handle and immediately shone the light on the spot where she thought she'd seen the figure.

Nothing was there.

It was just a... just a... She couldn't finish the thought, but since there seemed to be no present danger, she calmed slightly, and her attention returned to the jewelry box and future conversations with Jordan about commissions.

She scanned the top of the vanity with the flashlight. There was no sign of the necklace. She looked at the floor underneath. There it lay, only about an inch away from where the flashlight had fallen. She scooped it up as quickly and carefully as she could, stood up, and placed it in the bottom of the jewelry box as close to how she'd found it arranged as she could. "There you go."

She put the tray back in, closed the lid, and placed her fingers on the key to lock it, when she felt a deep chill on the back of her head, neck, arms, and down her spine. It was so much more intense than the open-refrigerator sensation she'd felt in the mansion's entryway the other day. It felt like an icy breeze had just blown through the bedroom, but she hadn't felt the movement of any air or heard the hinges creak with the doors swinging from the change in air pressure.

She instinctively stepped back and turned around with the flashlight aimed directly in front of her, fully expecting to see the shadow, or the hypothetical squatter from the other day with their hands on the doors, having swung them back and forth to create the breeze.

She was still completely alone.

She pointed the light to her right, then to her left, but found no one crouching to jump out at her. She aimed the light straight down the twin hallways, but saw no one in the midst of running away.

She waited for another second as if something else disturbing were about to jump out at her.

Nothing did.

She nodded. "Let's get outta here." She turned back to the jewelry box, locked it with its key, scooped it up in her arms, and carried it out while awkwardly keeping her flashlight steadily trained in front of her.

She exited the master bedroom, walked down the hallway from which she'd come, somehow missed the west-east one, and found she'd arrived at a tower. *Wait, is this the west tower or some other one?* Feeling panic start to set in, she tried to orient herself. *If this is the west tower, I just follow this hallway to the top of the staircase, right?* She continued, but saw no staircase. *Crap. No, that's not right. There was that weird angle at the top of the staircase. Two hallways branched off.* Sure enough, she soon came upon a small hallway intersecting the current west-east one. She followed it and arrived at the top of the staircase. *Thank God!* She hammered her feet down the stairs as quickly as she could manage without tripping. She breezed past Artemis and Apollo, and headed straight for the front doors.

9

Outside, it still looked twilight even though Katherine had only been in the mansion for about half an hour.

She fumbled to dig her phone out of her pocket so she could call Dean to ground her after what she thought she'd just seen. She managed to drag the device out with her fingertip. She slid it up the side of her pants and jacket till she could safely lay it on top of the jewelry box. She turned it on, but the little indicator painfully reminded her that she had no signal. She sighed out loud. "Oh my God! Fine!" She held the device in place on top of the box as she stumbled down the hill to the gate.

At her car, she opened the door and set down the jewelry box. She clicked off the flashlight and put it on the passenger seat, then set her phone next to it. She carefully moved the box down onto the floor in front of the passenger seat. She picked up her phone and checked the signal again, thankfully now finding it had two bars. She removed the rubber gloves, tossed them aside, and called Dean.

"You've been gone a while!" he said, trying to sound cheerful.

She got in. "Yeah, it was a whole thing." She firmly closed the door, fired up the car, and started down the road.

"See any more Caspers?"

She knew he was only teasing, and in good fun, but what she had seen, she couldn't explain. *Was it actually a person? Was it a reflection of, like, curtains or something? If it was a person, why didn't they say anything when I called after them?* She dared not conjecture the possibilities of what she suspected. That was just too creepy. She told Dean what was technically true. "No, no Caspers."

"Oh, thank God! Any squatters?"

"Nah. Just old junk I hope to sell."

"Oh? Good? You found some stuff?"

She told him all about the jewelry box with its goodies inside. That description alone, including the relevant details, likely histories of how and where the pieces had been crafted, and finally what she expected to make from them alone, took her the rest of the trip back to town.

Pulling up to her place, she excused herself, wished him well, and said goodbye. She then dialed Jordan.

THE HAUNTING OF BLACKSTONE MANSION

"Ms. Norrington, wonderful to hear your delightful voice again, but I thought I was clear before," he said.

"Mr. Blackstone, I can be at your place in an hour and a half. I need max ten minutes of your time. If I don't convince you to allow me to handle your estate by the end of that, then you won't have to file any charges 'cause I'll surrender *myself* to the police for two counts of trespassing on your family's private property."

He chuckled, very amused. "That's not necessary, Kathy. Wait, two counts?"

"Ten minutes. Max."

"I'll order sushi. You like sushi?"

"Love it."

"Any particular faves?"

"Yellow tail and red snapper. See you in ninety."

Katherine chose not to call Dean back for company on her trip all the way up to Portland. He hadn't done anything wrong. In fact, he was right; normally nothing ever shook her. But this time? The shadow in the shadows? The phantom moving cake stand? The strange perpetual twilight surrounding Blackstone mansion? The feelings of unease and dread she'd felt since the first time she'd stepped foot inside that entryway, which had only gotten worse with the last visit? None of it could she explain and none of it she wanted to hear Dean comment on.

So she turned on the car radio and tuned it to a local station as she gunned it as fast as the law would allow all the way up to Portland. Thankfully, with the pretty scenery and the lively folk music and bluegrass that the station was playing, the trip didn't feel that long.

Entering the city, she got on the interstate that eventually cut through the south of the main downtown area. She then cruised into the Pearl District and exited near Jordan's Vista building.

The Vista was a gorgeous high-rise, the tallest in the entire quarter, whose glass exterior reflected the park below and the sky above. She had to hand it to Jordan. By the look of things, he certainly didn't need the money that would come from her sale of his family's antiques. This little bit of show-and-tell was probably going to prove to be a significant challenge.

She parked a block away from the Vista, collected the jewelry box and her phone, and hiked over. She located Jordan's name on the building's directory and buzzed.

"You're late." Jordan sounded like he was trying to sound more impatient than he actually felt.

THE HAUNTING OF BLACKSTONE MANSION

"I'm right on time."

"Well, it *feels* like you're late."

She had no idea how to respond to such a ridiculous statement. "Um..."

"Come on up. While your sushi's still hot."

Was that a joke? Whatever, Kat. Let's just get this over with.

The door buzzed and she walked in. The elevator door was open so she stepped in. Again, she had to admire his surroundings. The normal floor-button panel was a touch screen. The motors driving the elevator's ascent were completely silent.

On exiting, she heard the muffled sound of beat-heavy electronic dance music. She found she was looking directly at Jordan's door. She approached it, took a quick breath, and knocked.

"Coming!" he called. Rushed steps preceded the sound of frantic fingertips wrestling with the doorknob.

The door opened wide. The music assaulted her ears. Before her eyes adjusted to the light, she saw a bright, wide view of the city and river below. *Wow, to wake up to that every morning. And I thought my mountain view was something special.*

Her eyes adjusting a little, she now saw a pristine white loft-style luxury condo. To her immediate right, two sets of perpendicular squishy couches sat in a sunken living area around a glass-shard firepit currently ablaze with dancing flames. To her left, she saw the edge of a granite countertop, what she imagined was only a small piece of a huge kitchen. On the wall to her right hung several items related to Jordan's DJ career. There were several gold records, a toy turntable, and a framed copy of some club announcement from Ibiza, Spain, featuring his DJ name.

Jordan held the door open. He wore a dark gray shirt that had clearly been tailored, but to a layperson it looked identical to any mid-range, store-bought button-down. His jeans were also obviously tailored, but had been carefully constructed with preworn patches on the kneecaps, to make them appear as though he'd worn them for a decade. His shoes were where he'd truly splurged. If she wasn't mistaken, they were not only custom-made, but by Santoni, one of the most exclusive shoemakers in Italy.

This was a man for whom not only everything had simply worked out, but upon whose predecessors fortune had smiled brightly, going back several generations.

Luckily for her, she'd met many, many people like Jordan, mainly millionaires, but some billionaires, so she was neither intimidated nor impressed by him. She, of course, wouldn't dare let on. If there was one thing she'd learned about the wealthy, it was that the only thing they loved more than being wealthy, was others' envy of that wealth.

"Mr. Blackstone?" she shouted over the music while she extended her hand.

Jordan called to the room. "Alexa! Music off!" The music ceased. Silence filled the air. "Please, Kathy. Jordan." He accepted her hand and shook it firmly.

She chose to understate her assessment of his abode. "Nice place."

His chuckle had an offended-sounding edge, as if he'd been expecting a far more dramatic reaction. "Thanks. Been here since it opened a few years ago. Please, come in." He got out of her way.

She walked in, past the living room area and kitchen, straight to the window. She looked down on the city below. *Ah, young wealth.* She turned to her right, getting a better look at the DJ paraphernalia. "Ibiza?"

"One of the best club towns in the world. That's from my first headlining gig, only my second ever."

She had no idea how to respond to that. "Nice."

"Your sush?"

"Sorry?" She faced him.

He'd gone to the kitchen and was currently holding up a plateful of sushi.

"Right. Forgot. Fantastic. Starving," she said.

He gestured to the couches. "Please, make yourself at home." He waited while she walked back to them.

She sat on the edge nearest the kitchen, set the jewelry box down on the opposite couch, and started to take off her jacket.

"Oh, let me, uh…" He ran over, took her jacket as soon as she'd removed it, and walked briskly back toward the front door. He opened a nearby door she hadn't noticed, behind which there was a walk-in closet, and hung up her jacket. He then returned to the kitchen, collected both their plates of sushi, and set them down on the edge of the firepit, her serving in front of her. "One more sec." He went to the kitchen, picked up a small dish of sauces and wasabi, and carried it back to their meal. "Wasabi imported from Tokyo."

She decided to test him, to push back a little on his towering mountain of confidence. "Really? Not Shizuoka?"

"Sorry?"

"I thought the most prized wasabi root was cultivated in Shizuoka."

"I've found that I prefer the Tokyo variety."

She scooped up two pieces, dipped them in Ponzu sauce, and gobbled them down. The fish was excellent. Or she was starving. Or both. "This is fantastic."

"Oughta be. Michelin-starred joint."

THE HAUNTING OF BLACKSTONE MANSION

He's not bringing up the mansion. Is he stalling so I waste my ten minutes? She suspected he wasn't that sleazy or cynical, but she still preferred to remain cautious. "So, Mr. Blackstone."

"Please, Kathy, I already told you. Jordan." He flashed the kind of winning smile that probably tended to get him whatever he damn well pleased. "I insist."

"Okay, Jordan, then since we're both insisting, Kat is fine."

"Kat?"

"Yeah."

"Not Kathy?"

"No."

"Or Anita?" The name he'd accidentally used over the phone the first time.

"Definitely not."

"You got it."

"So, Jordan, this is just one piece I found that, alone, is worth your time." She slid the jewelry box closer to him. "If you'll allow me to fill you in."

"Please, by all means."

"This is a jewelry box, as I'm sure you could tell. Almost certainly owned by your family's matriarch as it was located on her vanity next to the bed."

"Granny Gloria."

"Oh, was that her name?"

"If I have the timeline right. The last of the, as you said, matriarchs to actually reside in the mansion."

She realized that in her haste to attempt to assess the mansion's pieces and convince him to let her sell them, she hadn't actually put any real homework into the generation of the family who lived there. "Oh really?"

"Yep. After them, the family hightailed it, never went back. In fact, as far as I know, you're the first to set foot inside since the last person."

So the rumors are true! "You know what happened?"

"What do you mean?"

"Why your family just up and abandoned their stunning home? With everything left inside?"

He picked up a piece of sushi and shoved it in his mouth. He sat back and chewed while he considered her question. "I don't know. I guess I never really thought about it before. No one ever talked about it much. In fact"—he leaned forward again—"I don't remember anybody *ever* talking about it."

"Maybe I can find out more as I assess all the pieces."

He smiled. "Nice move, Kat, but we're not quite there yet. The box?"

"The box." She patted the top of the jewelry box. "So, Granny Gloria owned it, as you can see, highly skilled craftsmanship. She had it made, didn't buy it from a store. In fact, if you'll observe the tiny little imperfections of the silverwork on top, she had it handmade by a master craftsman. She loved this piece and loved what she put in it."

"I don't mean to sound dismissive..."

She nodded.

"But why does any of that matter?"

"That she had it custom-made?"

"All of it. I mean, it's a pretty jewelry box, right? Made out of, I assume, quality materials. So, whoever'd be interested in buying it, wouldn't that be it?"

"To a local pawnshop, yes, maybe, but to a collector, every piece of this box's story is important. What they're collecting is not just a jewelry box, not even just a finely crafted jewelry box. They're collecting Grandma Gloria's relationship to her belongings, her jewelry, her history with the house, with the family. I'll find someone who will love this box as much as she did."

He nodded slowly, looking like her words were sinking in.

"So, talking turkey, I expect the box alone, without the jewelry inside, could fetch you as much as fifty thousand dollars, given the materials, craftsmanship, and history."

He nodded again. "Not bad."

"However, lucky for you, we also have what she had, what she cherished, so even if you don't end up selling all of it together, the fact that she kept her prized jewels in here, that would be enough for the passionate collector."

"So, what do we have?"

"Interestingly, your many times great-grandmother had a thing for emeralds. There's a set of earrings, a set of bracelets, but the beast? That's the necklace at the bottom. A very impressive piece."

He pointed to the key sticking out of the box. "So do I just...?"

"One sec." She took the box of plastic gloves out of her purse and handed him a pair. "Please, Jordan, by all means."

He put on the gloves, pinched the key between his fingers and turned it carefully, just as she had, as if his very touch might break the box.

She placed another piece of sushi in her mouth, and lay back into the comfortable, squishy couch, and chewed slowly, savoring the taste, as she eagerly anticipated his blown-away reaction at seeing Grandma Gloria's breathtaking jewelry.

He lifted the lid and paused. "Um, Kat?"

"Yeah?"

"I don't understand."

"What do you mean?"

"Did you forget them?"

"What are you talking about?" She leaned forward to look into the box. Her jaw dropped open, spilling out a tiny bit of partially chewed fish.

THE HAUNTING OF BLACKSTONE MANSION

The box was empty.

The tray was still there, but both the set of earrings and bracelets were missing.

"No, I did *not* forget them," she declared, as she moved his hands aside and lifted the tray.

The necklace was gone.

"What in the hell?" she asked.

"You're sure you put the jewelry in the jewelry box?"

"Yes, I'm sure! I held that necklace in my own two hands!" She stood, marched out of the sunken area, to the window. Her eyes searched the surrounding building roofs as if they'd somehow fill her in on what had happened. *This isn't possible. I saw that jewelry in that box! I replaced the necklace after I dropped it on the floor!*

He chuckled to himself with a certain bitter edge. "I get it."

She turned around. "You get what?"

He stood. His winning smile had disappeared. He walked up the stairs from the sunken area, then stopped and gave her a little tilt of his head. "What, is it Mock-the-Trust-Fund-Baby Day?"

"What are you talking about?"

"You saw the mansion, you looked me up, you caught a few headlines, family finances not quite as strong as they used to be, and dangled that little selling-antiques carrot."

She could not believe her ears. "What?"

"You catch this all on your phone? For a 'gotcha' podcast? Got drones watching us from outside?"

She walked right up to him. "You honestly think I'd waste my time digging that jewelry box out of your however-many-great-grandparents' master bedroom, drive all the way up here, give you a dog-and-pony show just to, what? Grab a gotcha for a friggin' podcast?"

"Don't forget the free sushi."

"I swear to you that jewelry was in that box. I don't know what happened, but you let me rep your estate, I will not only dump a boatload of money at your front door, but I will also get to the bottom of whatever is going on here."

"Your ten minutes are up." He turned to step away from her.

She got in his way. "Am I repping your estate?"

"Kathy, we're done here." He headed toward the stairs leading up to his bedroom.

"Let me catalog one room, at my expense, auction those items, and show you what I can do."

He stopped, but didn't turn around.

"One room," she repeated.

"Your expense?"

She walked up right behind him. "When you see how much I can make, you will beg me to clear out the rest."

He finally faced her. "One room. One week. Now, if you'll excuse me, I'm sure you can let yourself out." He hiked up the stairs. He didn't turn around. "You have my number."

She sighed hard, but said nothing else. She returned to the firepit, collected the jewelry box, marched to the closet, retrieved her jacket, and left.

10

Katherine had gotten on the interstate and was currently heading back home. She punched in a number on her phone. The line rang twice.

"Hello?" Kirk asked.

"Kirk? It's Katherine."

"Oh, hey! Nice to hear from you. So, need some help with that flip?"

"Um, I haven't been a hundred percent honest with you. Can you meet in about an hour?" While she'd gunned it from Blackstone to get up to Portland in only an hour and a half to meet Jordan, she didn't particularly feel like breaking the speed limit all over again to meet Kirk in record time.

"Yeah"—he sounded very hesitant—"yeah, I can do that. Meet at Starbucks?"

"Perfect."

"I'll text you the address."

"Great. See you then." She hung up. After a few more seconds, her phone buzzed with the address to a Starbucks in Creek.

THE HAUNTING OF BLACKSTONE MANSION

She stared at her phone, then at the radio. For the first time in a long time, she didn't feel like reaching out to Dean, and she didn't feel like listening to music. Her mind was so abuzz with Jordan's challenge of a week to move, sort, catalog, and sell a room of his family's antiques, she couldn't really think about anything else. So she enjoyed the beauty of the Oregon countryside and the silence that came along with it.

"That's quite a story." Kirk sipped his matcha latte.

He and Katherine were seated at a pair of small sofas in the little Starbucks in his corner of town. She'd just finished telling him not only was she not renovating the house where she was staying, but she wasn't even renting the entire house. Then, of course, there was everything else, about the mansion and Jordan.

"Yeah," she said.

"I've got one question."

"Fire away."

"Why didn't you just tell me?"

She sighed hard. It was a perfectly reasonable question.

"I mean, if you don't wanna—" he said.

AUGUSTINE PIERCE

"No, it's fine. I dunno. I just—" She set her hot cocoa aside and leaned forward, rubbing her palms together for lack of anything else to do. "You ever experience something where, the thing wasn't terrible in and of itself, but because people asked you about it so much, you just didn't wanna answer anymore? Like, it's not their fault. For them, it's the first time asking, but you just don't wanna deal with it?"

"Oh yeah." He chuckled bitterly, took another sip of his tea, then set it aside. "My brother comes out a few years ago. Everyone's cool with it. The family's good. Even my old, conservative grandfather's like, 'Go get 'em, kid!' Everybody else, though? Neighbors? Teachers? Coaches? Every one of them practically corners me, and is like, 'Hey, what was it like? When Pete came out? Were you shocked?' After the fourth person asked me, and they asked me pretty much the same question, I just tossed them the answer, rapid-fire. 'Yes, Peter came out. No, I was not expecting it. Yes, I'm fine with it. No, I don't know if he has a boyfriend. No, he's not into Streisand.'"

She laughed at the perennial stereotype that all gay men were die-hard fans of Barbra Streisand.

He smiled at the memory. "So this person looks at me like, *Wow, you're a dick*, but the conversation ends."

"So it worked."

"It worked."

THE HAUNTING OF BLACKSTONE MANSION

"Well, my brother didn't come out. I don't have a brother, but yeah, I just didn't know how to explain it all without making it seem…"

"Strange?"

"Yeah, I guess. Forgive me for bold-faced lying to you?"

He rocked his head back and forth, feigning weighing the issue. "I mean, I guess that depends on whether you have an actual job for me and the boys."

"I do, but it's not fixing up a house to flip it."

"Okay."

"It does involve a house, though."

"With you so far."

"You know Blackstone mansion?"

"That's the creepy, old haunted house up the hill in Blackstone, right?"

"That's right." She went on to explain the deal she'd made with Jordan.

"So we're just moving furniture?"

"I mean, basically, yes, but it's very delicate furniture moving. A piece gets one scratch and the price goes down ten grand."

"That shouldn't be a problem. We can get plenty of Bubble Wrap, blankets, and all that. I'll tell my guys to be extra careful."

"Great."

"So where's the stuff going?"

AUGUSTINE PIERCE

That's a really good question, Kirk. "Um, I should have that squared away by the time we move it."

"So we go in, we pack up a room, carry it out, load it up, drop it off at whatever place, and that's it?"

"Pretty much."

"Okay, yeah, no problem. When you need this done?"

"I have a week, so could you guys do it, like, Wednesday, after work? I know it'd suck to work after working all day, but I may need the rest of the week to take care of everything else."

He nodded slowly.

She guessed the idea of working for hours after a day's work wasn't very appealing, but she could tell he also wasn't completely against it.

"Sure, why not? I got guys I can call," he said.

"Wow, great. So, what are we talkin'?"

"Uh, thirty bucks an hour by us four by probably six hours to keep it safe, so seven-twenty even."

"I can do that."

"You can pay us at the end. I trust you."

"Can you get necessary supplies, equipment?"

"What are we looking at?"

"Well, at least lights and Porta-Potties since there's no functioning electricity or plumbing."

"I'll figure it out."

"And, of course, gimme the receipts. I can reimburse you."

THE HAUNTING OF BLACKSTONE MANSION

"No problem."

"Right, so I guess meet at my place after you guys get off work, say, between six and seven? I'll text you my address."

He downed the rest of his tea. "I'll eagerly await your text." With that, he stood to go.

She walked with him out the door. They stopped between their cars.

She heard Dean's voice in her head: *Invite him over. Invite him over.*

He's gotta get back to work.

After, then.

We sleep together tonight, I have to work with him all night Wednesday, then pay him at the end? Kinda weird.

Pussy.

Shut up. "So, um, thanks for helping me out with this, and so last-minute."

"Not a problem, Kat. Anything to help a new arrival to the beautiful Pacific Northwest."

"All right, well, I guess you've gotta go."

"Yeah, gotta finish my shift. I mean, I could just take off, but Annie'd kill me. And they'd probably fire me."

"Well, we don't want that."

"No, we do not."

She clumsily stuck out her hand. "Till Wednesday."

He accepted her hand and shook it. "Till Wednesday."

They stood there for another awkward half a second, when she finally laughed and turned to her car. As she opened her door, she threw him a parting comment. "I'll text you."

"That'd be much appreciated." He walked around the front of his car and got in.

They pulled out of the parking lot and drove their separate ways.

You should've invited him over.

Shut up.

Closer to Blackstone, Katherine started debating on whether she should call Drew. *Technically, the living room's not my space, but if I tell him I'm using it, he'll probably wanna charge me. And then there's all the stuff around his dead father. Would he really care that I'm using the space where his dad used to live?* She sighed. *Yeah, he probably would.* "I won't tell him," she told the on-coming road. "What he doesn't know and all that."

She soon passed by Blackstone's town square, and a minute after that she was home. She grabbed her phone and scooped up the jewelry box. She carried

THE HAUNTING OF BLACKSTONE MANSION

them inside and set the box on the living room coffee table.

She spoke to the box. "First thing tomorrow morning, start rolling calls." She nodded her self-confirmation. *Now to pick a room.*

She wasn't immensely keen on returning to Blackstone mansion alone, especially as it was getting closer to nightfall, but now that she had that deadline, she needed to get going. First step was to choose which room she, Kirk, and his crew would tackle.

She jumped back in her car and started her drive out to the mansion. She again chose to listen to the silence of the road and surrounding woods as she talked herself through these next steps. "Better to be on the ground floor so we don't have to deal with any stairs. Also one of the rooms from the two hallways directly off the entryway so we minimize the distance. That narrows it down to, what, four rooms?"

She soon arrived at the mansion's gate. She armed herself with her flashlight and started the trek up the hill. She was so much more determined this time that she hardly noticed the hike or the eerie, perpetual twilight that loomed over the property.

She entered the house and clicked on her flashlight. The bright beam slicing through the shadows was immensely comforting. She felt like she was literally slaying the fears that she'd developed around the building, which had steadily intensified with each subsequent visit.

She took a breath and attempted to speak with solid authority. "All right, whoever's in here, I've got a job to do, and I was hired by your legit heir to do it, so any problem with me removing and selling your stuff, you take it up with him, 'cause it was ultimately his decision. Good? I don't mess with you, you don't mess with me. Got it?"

There was no answer. Not even a creak from a distant floorboard.

"Okay? We good? Lookin' at you two." She shone her light directly on each of Artemis's and Apollo's faces.

They did not react.

"I'm comin' in now."

Still no response.

"All right." She rolled her eyes. "So pathetic." *Wonder about that jewelry, the necklace, what happened to it.* "Worry about it later. Take care of this."

She entered the hallway to the left of the staircase. She walked to the first door and opened it wide. It looked very much like the other rooms she'd seen, but this one had several very large portraits hung on the walls. The first one she saw, on the opposite wall, was of a handsome young man, maybe twenty years old, dressed in British-style riding gear and standing next to a beautiful Andalusian. While he wasn't quite smiling, his countenance was bright with the confidence and cheer of someone who soon was to inherit a massive fortune. "Rich people and their horses."

She entered the room, hoping to find at least one work that was now considered a masterpiece. Maybe a Monet or a Picasso. An original of theirs would easily go for tens of millions, which would undoubtedly make Jordan very happy. But even someone like Munch would set Jordan up for the rest of his life.

She turned to her right, and her light soon fell on a new frame. Her adrenaline surged as she imagined what might be hanging there. When the frame came into full view, she recognized the image immediately. It was a landscape of Mt. Hood set on the distant horizon. She grumbled. *Not exactly Munch.* She guessed that Mr. Blackstone had ordered the painting from some local artist, someone probably almost as unknown then as he or she would be today. Such a choice for their gallery frankly felt a little kitschy for such a wealthy family. *Maybe Blackstone insisted on it to Gloria*.

The next frame contained the image of a lad a little younger than the first, probably around sixteen. He wore a top hat and navy blue suit as he stood next to a small table. It reminded Katherine of the ubiquitous portraits of European royalty, of similar style and composition that she'd seen in the Louvre in Paris. *Probably the Blackstones' attempt to portray their son as a modern-day prince.* She stepped closer to the portrait. Unlike that of his older brother, this boy's mouth was set in a straight line.

She moved on to the next one, another disappointment, as, far from being a masterpiece, it was Mr. Blackstone's turn to strike a pose. He leaned on a cane with his left palm, and his right hand rested on a rifle. Like his son standing next to the table, Mr. Blackstone wore a tall top hat and dark gray suit. *Wonder if he actually hunted or just played a hunter on TV.* She knew it was common in that era, as with many others, for men, especially the heads of wealthy families, to project an image not only of wealth, but of rustic masculinity, despite the fact that many of them would never have been caught dead outside their salons and smoking rooms, if they had any say in the matter.

She took a step closer to Mr. Blackstone's portrait. He had the rosy cheeks, waxed moustache, and frankly, the dorky grin creeping onto his lips that reeked of a man born into and swimming in wealth and privilege his whole life.

She reached the open doorway. Next to it hung a family portrait. By the looks of their poses and expressions, they'd had to stand there for quite a

THE HAUNTING OF BLACKSTONE MANSION

while. *Probably only, like, twenty minutes for the sketch, but I bet it felt like hours to them.* She circled her flashlight clockwise from the top. As with the previous portraits, Mr. Blackstone looked delighted, his older son looked cocksure, and his younger son looked like he was simply tolerating this whole affair. "What was going on there—?"

She froze when her eyes landed on Gloria. She wore a long, dark gray evening dress. Katherine raised her light up to Gloria's face. She also wore a smile, a tiny one, but it had the tight look of having been rehearsed and performed for years, if not decades. She was a stern-looking woman, not quite pretty, but hardly ugly either. "Did I see *you* in the master bedroom?" The image before her was so much more than what she thought she'd caught reflected in the surface of the necklace's largest diamond. And then the shadowy figure she thought she'd observed gliding away from the far side of the bedroom after she'd knocked over her flashlight. It did stand to reason, though, that if any ghost were haunting the master bedroom, keeping a close eye over the jewelry, it would be hers.

Katherine felt a shiver go down her spine and swung around, fully expecting to see Gloria standing right behind her.

No one was there.

AUGUSTINE PIERCE

Still, to feel safer, Katherine positioned herself between the open door and the family portrait. "All right, Gloria." She studied the woman's face, silently admiring her. Being a woman today was tough. She could only imagine what it was like then, even one of such prodigious means. *Probably had to rein in Mr. Blackstone a bunch.* She thought about showing Jordan the jewelry box. *Did Gloria hide that jewelry so that Jordan wouldn't see it, think I was an idiot, not let me sell this stuff?*

This was all sounding too crazy, even in her head. Ghosts weren't real. She hadn't seen Gloria's specter in the master bedroom. As for the missing jewelry, she must have misplaced it somewhere, somehow, when she wasn't paying attention. "I should go back up there when I'm done down here."

Satisfied that she'd seen all there was to see in here, and disappointed that this room wasn't worth hers or Kirk's effort, she exited and closed the door behind her.

Back in the hallway, she moved on to the next door. Opening it, her flashlight found gleaming metal highlights and the sheen of polished wood. Upon stepping in, she found an immense gun collection that spread across all four walls, with the obligatory sofas and chairs placed in the center of the room. "That's more like it." There were rifles, handguns, Tommy guns, arquebuses, muskets, and other firearms, all from prestigious manufacturers like Winchester, Colt, and Remington. It was clear that as the emerald jewelry was Gloria's pride and joy, these firearms were Mr. Blackstone's. "Gun collectors, antique collectors, or both." She allowed herself a satisfied smile, as, given the right collectors, these items would fetch Jordan probably just as much as a hypothetical Picasso from the portrait room.

That emerald jewelry. The curiosity was nagging at her. She knew she hadn't simply dropped or replaced it all. She knew something else had happened.

She took out her phone, went to the camera app, and proceeded to take plenty of pictures of this gun room that she could show Kirk and his boys, not to mention that she could e-mail to prospective collectors.

After snapping a good dozen or so, she dropped her phone back in her pocket, exited into the hallway and finally into the entryway.

The necklace. I held the necklace!

She was almost at the front doors, reaching her hand out to grip the left one's knob, when she halted. *I know I didn't misplace them!* It would only take a second. She'd run upstairs, down the hallways, stick her head in the master bedroom, confirm that the jewelry was on the floor or whatever, scoop it up to sell with the jewelry box, and get out of here.

She turned back to the staircase and raced up, barely keeping her flashlight on the space in front of her. When she reached the top, she booked down the hallways straight to the master bedroom. She awkwardly slid the flashlight farther down her wrist, gripped the double doorknobs, and opened the doors wide so she could make a sweeping search with her light.

She aimed the light to her left, then, like a camera tripod, turned a full 180 degrees. There was no sign of the jewelry, on tables or under them.

Then her light met the bed.

"Wait." She hesitated with her flashlight aimed right on the edge of the burgundy curtain. She slowly moved the light to the right. The flowing curtain hung over every square inch of the bedchamber's interior. "Wasn't that curtain open the last time I was up here?" She took out her phone and frantically scrolled through the photos. "Oh my God." There it was clear as day from the first picture she'd taken of the room.

The bed's curtains were open.

A tingle ran up and down her spine. Someone had since closed these curtains. But who and for what reason, she had no idea.

THE HAUNTING OF BLACKSTONE MANSION

She hadn't seen the jewelry anywhere on the floor or on a surface. And that damned four-poster bed with its hanging burgundy curtains was a giant gift box on Christmas morning. She could not resist it. *I'll just take one peek. I'll throw it back and do a quick sweep with the flashlight. Confirm there's nothing there.* Or no one.

Her heart started pounding so hard she could feel her whole body pulse. She stretched her arms out and widened her stance, her best attempt at being ready for an attack. She took slow, determined steps to the side of the bed. Reaching it, she took a deep, concentrated breath, gripped the curtain with her left hand, and held the flashlight steady with her right. She hoped, at a minimum, to momentarily blind whoever might be lying there, so she could buy herself enough time to run like hell out of the house.

All right. Count of three. One...

She flipped the curtain open.

No one was in there.

She frantically swung the flashlight left and right, as if she'd somehow missed the hiding intruder.

Nothing.

Except for a tiny glint. It was the smallest little sparkle. It had appeared at the bottom of her peripheral vision. At the bottom. As if lying in the bed.

Look down. Her heart began to race again. She slowly lowered the light.

Dozens of sparkling lights filled her vision. Pointing the flashlight at the roof of the bed, she diminished the harsh sparkles to a mellow glow of white and green.

Emerald.

She realized she was staring at Gloria's diamond-and-emerald necklace. But it wasn't just the necklace. As she turned her gaze to the left, she found the bracelets. To the right, the earrings. But that wasn't the strangest part. Leaning back, taking in the whole display, she realized the jewelry had been placed on the bed where Gloria would have slept, each piece placed exactly where she would have worn them had she worn them to bed.

The tingle that Katherine had felt down her spine was nothing compared to the chill she felt now.

She swung around. No one was there. She pointed the light across the room. No one was there either. She ran around the bed to the vanity. The chair was empty. As far as she could tell, she was completely alone in this room. And yet someone had located Gloria's jewelry, placed the pieces on the bed exactly where she would have slept, and had drawn the curtains, the perfect present for Katherine to find.

THE HAUNTING OF BLACKSTONE MANSION

She stood still and caught her breath. She felt surrounded. Yet nothing was there but the quiet and the shadows.

She gripped the curtain and lifted it. She allowed herself another look at the jewelry, let her flashlight's beam rest on the necklace, and admired its sparkling beauty. *The box'll be worth so much more.*

She set the flashlight on the vanity, removed her jacket, bent over, scooped the bracelets and necklace into her coat, and rolled it up. She then palmed the earrings and carefully slid them into her pants pocket. *Not the best place, but short notice.*

She grabbed her flashlight and marched straight out of the master bedroom, through the hallways, down the staircase, and out the front doors.

Without her jacket on, it was noticeably colder. *Whatever. Gotta carry this stuff back.* Thinking of the jewelry, about how it had so recently managed to hide itself, she stuck her hand in her pocket. The earrings were still there. She unrolled her jacket enough to where she saw the glint of one of the bracelets. *Check and check. Let's get outta here.*

She walked down the road to the gate, jumped in her car, placed her jacket on the floor on the passenger side, and set off.

On the way back, she wrestled between wanting to get the mystery of Gloria's jewelry out of her head and obsessing over it. *Where was it? Who put it there?*

AUGUSTINE PIERCE

Jordan's the only one who knew I was even looking at it. Did he drive all the way down from Portland just to set that up to mess with me? Of course not. That was ridiculous. But after crossing that possibility off the list, what remained was even more unbelievable.

When she arrived at the house, she immediately put her jacket on the coffee table, sat next to it, unrolled it, and gasped in relief that the bracelets and necklace were still there. She proceeded to replace them in the jewelry box, then dug into her pocket, took out the earrings, and put them back in their rightful place.

She stood and closed the jewelry box with an emphatic grunt. "Stay."

She went to the kitchen, made herself a completely uninspired dinner of spaghetti, slurped that up at the kitchen table, cleaned up, and retired to her bedroom where she plugged in her phone and passed out during a documentary on the life and times of the Medici family, the most prominent of the Italian Renaissance.

11

Katherine woke up before her alarm went off. She had a fire in her belly not only because Jordan had given her a deadline, but because for the first time since having moved to Blackstone, she was in her element.

She had barely finished getting dressed when she made her first call to Miles Holbrook in London. She'd known Miles for years and had done a lot of business with him. He had far deeper contacts than she did in the various European markets. If a piece could be sold in those markets, he was the one to do it.

"Kat! It's great to hear from you! How are things?" Miles asked.

"Miles, how are you? Listen, I know it's already evening over there, but I thought you'd be interested in some of the finest Winchesters and Colts I've ever seen. The private collection of stupidly wealthy industrialist Mr. Blackstone."

"Winchesters and... Where are you?"

AUGUSTINE PIERCE

"Blackstone, Oregon."

"I'm sorry, I don't know where that is. Is that near Canada?"

She chuckled. "Not quite. Listen, I'm sending you some pics. You're gonna wanna send someone out here, or better yet, send yourself."

After some more pleasantries with Miles and a bit more hype to get him excited, she ended the call just as he was at his most exuberant. She next called Aleeyah Morgan in New York.

"Kat Norrington! It has been too long, darling," Aleeyah said in her crisp, upper-class New England accent. Katherine had met Aleeyah randomly at a gallery showing many years ago, and they'd hit it off as they both commented on how much they'd hated the art that was on display. Aleeyah mostly dealt in fine art and mostly ran in very exclusive circles, but among those exclusives, she knew a number of very wealthy gun collectors. "How are you? How's it been since—"

"Great, Leeyah, just taking a little break in rural Oregon."

"That's what I'd heard. You're in some little hamlet called White Rock, aren't you?"

"Blackstone."

"Of course. That's what it was. And how is it in Blackstone? Enjoying the fresh, Oregonian air?"

THE HAUNTING OF BLACKSTONE MANSION

"Actually, Leeyah, I recently happened upon a stash of something that you are going to be very interested in."

"Oh, do tell, Kat, do tell!"

All Katherine had to do was say the words "antique" and "Winchester" and Aleeyah was all over it.

"And you're telling me these pieces are authentic period firearms?" Aleeyah asked.

"Saw them myself. I'll text you some pics. But you'd better get out here."

"I will catch the next flight."

"Eh, maybe give it a day. I'm still wrapping things up."

"You text me, I'll be there."

Katherine soon got off the phone with Aleeyah and on to her next call. This one was to Chase Fredericks, based in Los Angeles. He was pretty much a living stereotype of LA's entertainment culture. He was very handsome, if short, and he always wore very expensive jackets, but never with ties. The best thing about him was that he knew all the rich producers and actors, many of whom loved guns, even if they never would have admitted so publicly. She hadn't done as many deals with him, but figured having him to play off the others was a good idea.

"Katie! Great to hear your voice! Heard you trotted off to Washington." Chase was the only one among her friends, acquaintances, and family who ever called her Katie.

"No, Oregon."

"What's in Oregon?"

"Trees mostly. And coffee."

"Coffee's always good."

"So, Chase, I recently happened upon a huge cache of antique firearms. Think any of your people would be interested?"

"Firearms? Antique? How old we talkin'?"

"I mean, the collection ceased in the nineteen twenties, so older than that."

"Huh. That could be interesting. You called that Limey prick?"

"If you're referring to Miles, yes."

Chase chuckled. "Well, if ol' Miles is in, I gotta check it out."

"I'll text you when. Still putting things together."

"Look forward to it!"

"Same here."

"Listen, Katie, I got a thing, but we'll talk!" He hung up.

Feeling particularly giddy, she announced to her bedroom, "I'm gonna celebrate!" She knew her words were premature, but even without any actual sales, this was feeling right already.

She got showered, dressed, ran downstairs, and paused at the coffee table, half surprised to see Glo-

THE HAUNTING OF BLACKSTONE MANSION

ria's jewelry box still dutifully sitting there. She ran out the door and almost jumped in her car when she remembered the diner was within walking distance, and she felt like enjoying this fine morning.

She took a very nice fifteen-minute stroll in the crisp morning air with the sweet song of birds all around her. She realized that hearing birds now sounded strange after having spent so much time on the mansion's grounds during the last few days, where she heard no birds at all. *Wonder why that is.*

At the town square, the trees were looking particularly green, and the mountain was looking more majestic than ever. She regarded it with a certain satisfaction, as if she'd come to this little town to conquer the mountain and knew she was about to do so.

She arrived at the diner and pushed the door open so enthusiastically that she heard the bells bounce repeatedly against it.

Wendy greeted her with a smile. "'Morning, hon. What can we get you?"

When does she not work here? "'Morning. I need to see one of those dessert menus." She took a seat and Wendy placed one in front of her. Katherine opened the menu to double check her choices. Her eyes immediately went to the key lime pie. They then drifted down to the chocolate cake. *I mean, why not?* She set the menu down.

Wendy joined her. "So, what'll it be?"

"The pie. And the cake. Oh and some hot cocoa, too, please."

Wendy smiled. "Of course. Comin' right up."

Katherine dug out her phone and called Dean. It took him a second to answer.

"Hey, what's up? Haven't heard from you in a bit."

"I know. Sorry."

Wendy dropped off her pie, cake, and cocoa.

Katherine whispered to Wendy, "Thanks." She then spoke to Dean. "I've actually been busy, believe it or not."

"I don't, but go on."

"So that mansion?"

"The haunted one?"

She winced at his recollection, most likely his making fun of her experience there. "Yeah."

"Found more ghosts."

Actually, Dean... But she knew she didn't want to get into that with him. "Even better."

"Zombies?"

"No, D, come on."

"All right. Sowwy."

"The place is swimming with antiques. Like stuffed!"

"I take it you spoke with Jordan."

"Yeah."

"And it went well?"

"Pretty good. Yeah. Point is, he gave me that deadline? Well, I already called a few people, including Miles and Aleeyah."

"Didn't they...?"

"Yeah."

"So, won't this get a little awkward?"

"Awkward enough to drive up the price."

"You're terrible."

"I know. Anyway, I got some guys to move it all, the people to buy it, so..."

"So you're not gonna starve in rural Oregon!"

"Looks like it."

"Yay, Kitten!"

"To celebrate, I'm having pie *and* cake."

"And, of course, hot cocoa."

"Of course."

"I'll let you get to it."

"'Kay. Talk soon."

"Kisses." He hung up.

She dug into her pie first. It was pretty good. It tasted like the cook had mixed in a little too much crust and too little pie with too little key lime.

After she finished her celebratory sweets, she went back to the house and lay back on her bed while watching a documentary on Genghis Khan. *Man, like, how does one conquer that much, screw that much, and not keel over from a heart attack?* Once the initial presales and post-sugar buzzes wore off, she passed out. When she woke up, it was midafternoon and she found she had a text from Kirk.

> Still on for tomorrow? Address?

> Absolutely.

She sent her address.

> Great! See you tomorrow evening.

> See you then.

She set her phone aside, turned the documentary back on, and promptly passed out. She woke up a few hours later and it was already dark. She decided to take a long walk around Blackstone's downtown after which she came home, made some dinner, and retired to the bedroom and her laptop where she wrote and rewrote a list of all the things she'd do with her incoming commission. First, it consisted of things like "buy really nice desk," then it expanded to "take ski vacation on Mt. Hood."

She realized that taking a solo one felt a little sad, so she thought of somehow inviting Kirk, even though that'd be pretty intense for a first date. *Ah, ski-lodge sex.* It was with these pleasant fantasies swimming in her head that she finally crashed for the night.

12

Katherine was again up before her alarm was set to go off a little past seven. Today was an exciting day. While it would probably take all night, she knew by the end, she'd have all of Mr. Blackstone's guns and miscellaneous furniture from that first-floor room safely moved into her living room, ready to be shown off to her prospective buyers.

She spent the day switching between making food, watching documentaries on Julius Caesar, Caesar Augustus, and Alexander the Great, and checking up on some of the buyers her contacts knew.

One of Miles's buyers was a millionaire who lived in an actual castle in the Czech Republic. She knew he was more into weapons in general than specifically guns, but she hoped the age and history of the Blackstone items would intrigue him.

One of Aleeyah's friends was a New York hedge-fund manager who liked to go hunting on the weekends. While Katherine didn't know whether he was into antique guns, she figured if he was into the one, he'd be into the other.

One of Chase's buddies—to be fair, Chase called everyone buddy—was a very wealthy producer of some film franchise that she'd never seen. Something to do with flashy cars and lots of really hot women. He was one of those people who gave tons of money to the Democratic Party, but he also loved guns.

She had barely returned from her latest walk when the doorbell rang. She ran downstairs and answered it.

Outside, Kirk and three other guys were there, all bundled up, with four separate pickup trucks parked behind them.

"Good evening!" Kirk said.

"'Evening, guys," Katherine greeted. "Wanna come in, get a little warmed up before we have to go?"

"Sounds good." Kirk stepped aside and ushered his guys in, then closed the door behind them.

The four men hovered awkwardly next to the front door as Katherine fussed about in the kitchen.

"Coffee, anyone?" she asked.

"That'd be great," said the guy next to Kirk. He wore a puffy blue coat and a goatee.

"Love some," said the guy behind, who wore a jean jacket and full beard.

"Only way I can function this late," said the final guy, who wore a brown coat and was clean-shaven.

"Yeah, Shane usually works the morning shift, so this is a bit late for him," Kirk explained.

"Well, thanks for coming, Shane." Katherine gathered the four mugs as the coffee brewed.

"I'm sorry. Manners. This is Shane, you already met him, Dennis, and Randy." Kirk pointed to each of them.

Katherine stepped away from the kitchen and shook their hands. "Katherine. You guys can call me Kat. And thanks for helping me tonight."

"Not a problem," Shane said.

"All good," Dennis said.

"Happy to help," Randy said.

Katherine went back to the kitchen, poured the guys their coffee, and handed them out. They all thanked her.

"So, were you able to figure out your storage situation?" Kirk asked.

"You, sir, are looking at it." Katherine presented the living room with open arms.

"Okay." Kirk nodded.

"This gonna be enough space?" Shane asked.

"I hope so, 'cause this is what we've got," Katherine said.

"How long you have to keep the items here?" Dennis asked.

"Well, buyers are already flying out, so not long, I hope."

"We should probably get to it," Kirk suggested.

"You're right. You boys ready?"

Randy, Dennis, and Shane nodded. They took last sips of their coffee and dropped their mugs off on the kitchen counter.

"Right there is fine," Katherine confirmed.

"We following you, or did you wanna ride with?" Kirk asked.

Shane and Randy threw him a little grin.

"Yeah, I'm taking my car. Just in case we need any more space," Katherine said.

Kirk nodded and led the guys back outside. "Saddle up!"

Katherine followed right behind, closed and locked the door, then got into her car. She led the four pickups out of town and onto Promontory. They soon arrived at the mansion's gate. She parked in her usual spot just to the right of it. The other four parked on both sides of the road several yards behind her.

She got out and held up her phone. "You'll find these probably aren't gonna work so well."

Shane was already checking his phone. "Yeah, I see that. I assume there's no signal all over the hill."

THE HAUNTING OF BLACKSTONE MANSION

"I don't think so. If you need to call anybody, you'll probably have to walk a bit farther down the road."

"Dude, that gate is legit!" Dennis declared. "Who were these people? Billionaires?"

"In their day, probably."

"So we just waltz in?" Kirk asked.

"Yeah." Katherine walked up to the gate and pushed the right door open as wide as it would go.

Shane asked Kirk directly, "You sure we got permission to be up here?" He eyed the mansion's direction very suspiciously.

"We're good to go," Katherine replied. "We're here on the owner's permission."

"You got that in writing?" Shane asked.

"Um, I mean"—Katherine looked down the hill as if she were about to have to run down and make a call to Jordan—"I can call Jordan if you want."

"That won't be necessary," Kirk informed Shane. He then offered Katherine a smile. "We're all good."

"Great, let's head up." Katherine beckoned the guys to follow her up the road.

"How far is it?" Shane asked.

"Not far." Katherine gave him a polite, if forced, smile. From that point on to the loop, she felt pressure to get this hike over with now that Shane had already complained about it. With her added speed, and their having no problem keeping up, the trip only took about a minute.

Randy peered up at the mansion. "Wow."

At night, the house was a solid-black box topped with three triangular silhouettes against the swaying leafy limbs of the surrounding forest.

"Yeah, no way," Dennis concurred.

"We're only moving out one room of that thing?" Shane asked.

"Today, yeah." Katherine opened the right front door for them. "If I need to move more, I'll definitely let you guys know." She took her flashlight out of her purse and clicked it on. Pointing it inside, she stepped out of their way to let them in.

As they passed by her, they each gasped out loud. She was guessing that this was the first honest-to-goodness mansion they'd ever set foot in. She wasn't far behind, having only seen the inside of a handful, not including museums.

"This is friggin' huge!" Shane exclaimed from deep inside the entryway.

Kirk paused as he passed by Katherine, whispering, "Sorry about Shane. He's got some trust issues."

"Don't we all?" Katherine smiled.

Kirk nodded and smiled back, then headed in.

"Who are they?" Randy asked.

Katherine saw that he was pointing at the twin statues. "Those are Artemis and Apollo."

THE HAUNTING OF BLACKSTONE MANSION

"I don't see name plates," Shane said.

"I recognized them."

"Man, these guys *must've* been billionaires," Dennis said.

Once the guys had gotten over their initial shock, Katherine led them to the room. "So we are gonna be in there."

Randy eagerly stepped inside.

"Remember," Katherine reminded, "one nick and a piece loses value, so be extra careful."

Randy nodded. "Yes, ma'am." He threw the door open.

"Damn!" Dennis said.

"Nice!" Shane said.

"Seriously, dude"—Randy came out and informed Kirk—"you gotta check this stuff out!"

"Right behind you."

He and Katherine entered the room. They found the other guys all hovering with saucer-wide eyes at the artillery before them.

Shane nearly tripped over a sofa.

"Shane, careful!" Kirk insisted.

"Sorry, yeah, sorry." Shane spun around, faced the piece, and patted his hands over it as if to reassure it.

"As you guys can see, there's a lot," Katherine said. "I was thinking couches, tables, chairs, that stuff first, then on to the firearms."

The guys all nodded and grunted their agreement.

"Let's get the lights, generators, Porta-Potti," Kirk said.

"I'll get the dolly," Randy said.

"I guess we can start moving stuff out. You good with that, dude?" Dennis asked Shane.

Shane was still admiring one of the rifles. "Yeah, that's fine." He finally turned to see what Dennis was referring to, then joined him at the other end of a sofa.

"And I will get out of your guys' way," Katherine said with a grin. She retreated to the entryway.

Even with two of the guys in a room only feet away and two others heading down the hill, at most, several yards away, she felt suddenly and intensely alone. She peered at the door that had ultimately led her to the kitchen, to that cake stand that had mysteriously turned so extremely cold to the touch so quickly.

Dennis and Shane, both wearing rubber gloves, walked a sofa out of the room into the entryway, set it down, and went back for more furniture.

Katherine moved a few feet closer to the front doors, partly to get more out of their way, and to cast her gaze to the top of the staircase. She thought about her little experiences in the master bedroom.

THE HAUNTING OF BLACKSTONE MANSION

"Incoming!" Kirk announced as he approached the front doors carrying a set of four lamps.

Katherine got out of his way, and he went straight into the room. She then heard repeated squeaking and turned to find Randy dragging a large dolly up the front steps. It was piled high with a Porta-Potti and a machine that she guessed was the generator. She watched him as he joined the others.

The room lit up with a warm glow. A second light followed that made the room even brighter. A third and fourth made it light up like the sun was shining from within.

Katherine clicked off her flashlight, put it in her purse, walked over to the room's doorway, and peered in. Under very bright lights, the guys were all hard at work moving more furniture, setting up supplies of tape, Bubble Wrap, and blankets, or surveying the space, probably for potential challenges.

Since she knew they were in their element and didn't want to distract them or get in their way, she backed out into the entryway and walked outside.

She admired the view of the woods all over the hill, as much as she could see in the darkness. To her right, through breaks in the trees, she saw the mountain. She had to admire the Blackstone family for having built their dream house up here. Of any place nearby to build such a beautiful home, this was it.

AUGUSTINE PIERCE

"Pardon us, ma'am," Randy announced from right behind her.

She turned around, saw him and Dennis on either side of that first large sofa, which was riding gently on the dolly, and got out of their way. She stepped several feet to the side and watched them negotiate the front steps. Kirk hadn't been kidding about their professionalism. Randy and Dennis were very coordinated in their careful effort to get this sofa down the hill. But their work was slow, and Katherine could easily see how this one room would probably take the rest of the night.

She watched them roll the sofa down the hill. She nodded in satisfaction that only days ago she'd hardly finished pulling into the town, and now she was about to make herself some honest money.

Lacking anything else to do, with several hours to go, and not able to call Dean from up here—besides not wanting to bother him as much as she usually did—she dug out her phone, switched it on, and launched *Fruit Ninja*. She got down to the serious business of slicing fruit for points.

She wandered around the front of the mansion, its carriage loop, stayed out of the guys' way, and sliced fruit for level after level and until the game easily defeated her, and it was back to square one.

She was standing at the far end of the loop from the house and had just sliced open a bomb in *Fruit*

THE HAUNTING OF BLACKSTONE MANSION

Ninja, seriously crippling her game, when she heard Kirk call her.

"Hey, Kat?" he asked.

She looked up.

"Furniture's done. We should all take a look at the guns."

"Right. Be there in one sec." She put away her phone and walked to the front doors. Inside, Randy, Dennis, and Shane were all taking a sitting break on the bottom steps of the staircase.

Kirk nodded at the gun room. "After you."

Katherine entered and let out a tiny, involuntary gasp on seeing how open the space looked without the furniture.

"Right?" Kirk asked. "So much bigger. And it was already pretty damned big."

Randy, Dennis, and Shane had joined them. They silently admired their handiwork.

Katherine looked over the many guns on the walls. "While I'm not the world's foremost expert on the handling of firearms, we should be very, very careful, especially since these are antiques."

"And some may still be loaded," Kirk said.

Katherine looked back at him and nodded. *Hadn't thought of that. Who knows how careful Mr. Blackstone was with his guns?* "Maybe pick a wall, take from the middle, work our way down, then up, rinse, repeat?"

"Seems about right. Boys?"

AUGUSTINE PIERCE

His friends got to work on the wall opposite the open door. Randy and Shane stood on either side of a rifle that hung halfway up the wall. They cradled it in both hands, lifted it up, and gently away from the wall.

"Kat? A second?" Kirk asked.

Katherine followed him out to the entryway, almost to the front doors.

"In about an hour, you probably wanna head into town, pick up some sandwiches and stuff," Kirk suggested.

"Right. Dinner. I totally forgot," she said.

"I mean, I told them to be ready, so they all brought something, but ya know, growing boys."

"Also help me burn some time."

"Exactly. Don't want you to have to stand around bored all night."

"Just most of the night." She smiled.

"Right."

"Yeah, good call. In fact"—she threw a glance in the direction of the gun room—"maybe I'll head out now and just take my time."

"Even better."

"Are they gonna be good handling all that?"

"I promise I will make sure."

"Even Shane?"

"Even Shane. Promise. Go take your time."

THE HAUNTING OF BLACKSTONE MANSION

"Thanks." She walked out and headed down the hill toward her car. She took her time driving back to town, which, unfortunately, even with going slower, took only about ten minutes longer than usual.

13

Katherine went to the little grocery store and picked up armfuls of sandwiches, sliced cheese, crackers, jerky, and juices. At the counter, she dumped it all into as much of a pile as she could manage. "Sorry. It's a bit much."

The cashier nodded. "'S okay." He started swiping the items. "Need a bag?"

"Yeah, that'd be great."

He reached under the counter and took out exactly one bag that looked about the size of his fist, like it would hold one sandwich and maybe one juice bottle. He started stuffing it. Sure enough, only a sandwich, a juice bottle, and a package of jerky fit.

"Maybe a few more?" she asked.

He looked at her like she was speaking French, then reluctantly took out more bags.

When she emerged from the store, she now had six bags slung along her arms. She wrangled the bags as she opened the passenger side, and dumped them on the floor. Closing the door, she checked the time. It had only been about thirty-five minutes. She sighed. "Great. How to blow more time?"

She got in the car and drove to the south side of the town square. She parked, got out, and walked to the middle. There she sat on a bench, looked up at the mountain, and remained there for a quiet moment. *Admiring the mountain's not gonna burn much time either. If only they had a duck pond and I had bread crumbs.* She looked around the square, but neither a pond nor ducks appeared. *Damn it.* She pulled out her phone and dove into another game of *Fruit Ninja*. After a few rounds, she was sure some time had passed. She checked. Ten more minutes. She chuckled to herself. "All right. I'll just go back, take my time."

She returned to her car, got in, and set off for the mansion. Really taking her time stretched the journey to a good half hour. On pulling up to the gate, she found one pickup packed with skillfully wrapped furniture. As she got out of her car, she saw Kirk and Dennis exit the gate, carrying a wrapped rifle.

Kirk nodded. "Great timing. Almost time for dinner."

Katherine smiled. "Look at me with my timing."

As Kirk and Dennis placed the gun in the bed of another pickup, she opened her passenger side. "If you guys wanna grab a couple bags, we can get them in one trip."

Kirk and Dennis joined her, and she handed them each two bags of goodies.

"Teriyaki. Nice," Dennis said.

"I aim to please," Katherine said.

They walked together up the road to the mansion.

"How's it going?" Katherine asked.

"Good," Kirk said. "Should be done around 11:00, maybe a little after."

"Great! Then we can drive straight to my place, drop it all off, go to the ATM, and I'll get you guys your cash."

"Cash! Woo-hoo!" Dennis grinned and thrust a fist in the air.

Katherine chuckled. So did Kirk.

They reached the front doors and again found Randy and Shane taking a sitting break on the staircase's bottom steps.

Randy noticed the others' armfuls of bags. "What'd you bring us?"

"We got goodies, boys!" Kirk announced.

They all sat on and in front of the steps. Katherine, Kirk, and Dennis passed out snacks. Randy and Shane eagerly dug in. Once everything was passed out, Katherine happened to notice that she'd only gotten herself a sandwich and a bottle of juice. It

THE HAUNTING OF BLACKSTONE MANSION

was hardly enough for dinner. She'd have to make herself something more when she got home.

Kirk must have noticed how little she had as he handed her his sandwich. "Looks like you're a little low."

"Oh no, I'm fine," she said. "Those are for you guys."

"You didn't have dinner."

"I can always go back down."

"Twenty minutes there and back? Come on. Take it."

Katherine smiled and accepted the extra sandwich. She took a huge bite. *Guess he's right. One sandwich wouldn't have been enough.*

She noticed a rhythmic tapping and looked to her left. Kirk was playing the floor like a drum set with his fingertips. "You were doing that at the rental place."

Kirk stopped his little performance. "What?"

"Your 'drumming.'" Shane held up air quotes.

"Oh yeah, that. Sorry. Was it bothering you?"

Katherine shook her head. "It was good."

"He used to be a drummer," Shane said.

"Used to be?" Kirk sounded like he was trying to not take offense.

"Didn't you used to play in that band, the, uh, what was it called?" Randy asked.

"The Flippers?" Dennis asked.

"Dolphins," Kirk corrected.

"Shit name for a band, dude," Shane offered.

"Don't know what to tell you, man."

"You still play?" Katherine asked.

"You mean other than with himself?" Randy chuckled.

"Occasionally. Unfortunately, drumming doesn't quite pay the bills," Kirk said.

"Didn't you have a gig, like, two weeks ago?" Dennis asked.

Kirk simply nodded.

"I'd love to hear you play." Katherine immediately regretted how fan-girly she sounded.

"I'll text you with our next gig." Kirk sounded like he desperately wanted this portion of the conversation to end.

"I'd love to go."

After gulping some juice, Shane wiped his mouth on his sleeve and asked Katherine, "So, how much you think you're gonna get for all this stuff?"

"Shane." Kirk's tone had a note of harshness.

"It's fine," Katherine reassured Kirk, then answered Shane, "Honestly, I don't know. It's not like there's a set price."

"How much do you think?" Shane asked.

"That's none of our business," Kirk warned.

"It's okay," Katherine said. "How much do you think it's worth?"

"I dunno," Shane said. "Antique guns, assuming they still work, ten grand a piece by, how many, thirty?"

"I think fifty," Randy said.

"There are fifty guns in there?" Katherine asked.

"I didn't count, but yeah, a lot," Kirk said.

"Let's meet in the middle, say forty guns. So forty by ten, that's..." Shane trailed off trying to handle the mathematics.

"Four hundred thousand," Dennis said.

Randy whistled.

"And that's not counting the furniture," Shane said.

"Also not counting I'll be selling to people who will be selling to collectors. Collectors are willing to pay a lot for the right piece in the right condition," Katherine informed them.

"Wait, so you're saying that room's gonna sell for *more* than four hundred thousand?" Shane asked.

"A lot more."

"Man, I am in the wrong business!" Shane laughed, then asked Katherine, "How much of that's yours?"

Kirk stood. "Shane, why don't we take a walk?"

"I'm sorry, I'm sorry. I take it back. Never mind."

Kirk pointed at him, then turned his wrist and beckoned him.

With a dramatic groan, Shane stood and started for Kirk's side.

As he passed by, Katherine asked him, "Hey, Shane? How much you pull down in a year?"

"Good year? Forty K."

Katherine looked up at him and grinned. "More than that."

Shane grinned right back. "Touché, lady. Touché."

As Kirk and Shane walked away, Shane looked back at Katherine and mouthed, "Sorry."

Katherine smiled and held up an okay sign.

In another few minutes, they'd all finished their snacks, Kirk and Shane had returned from their walk, and it was back to work. As the guys packed and loaded the firearms, Katherine took pictures of the nearest rooms, being careful not to wander beyond that, went outside where she took walks up and down the road to the mansion, went to her car where she took a nap, but then as Kirk had predicted, the day was almost done around 11:00.

The group all met in the now stripped gun room. The floor and walls were completely bare. It looked almost as if no one had ever set foot in this room.

Katherine was very impressed with their work. "Wow. Great job, guys."

"Please leave a five-star review," Dennis said.

Katherine giggled.

THE HAUNTING OF BLACKSTONE MANSION

"Now we just gotta pack up, and it's back to Blackstone," Kirk said.

"Time to get paid!" Shane announced.

Kirk, Randy, and Dennis glared at him.

"What? I'm happy," Shane said quietly.

"Then I will get out of your guys' hair." Katherine waltzed out to the entryway and out the front doors.

A minute later, all four men came out carrying the lights, generator, and Porta-Potti.

"All good," Kirk informed Katherine.

"Fantastic." She happily started down the road with them.

When they reached the gate, the guys had to take a few seconds to negotiate the lights through the gate's doors. As she waited for them, Katherine looked admiringly back at the mansion.

There was a lone, rotating, flickering light in the top left corner. It looked like the world's meekest lighthouse in the middle of the forest.

"What the hell?" Katherine asked quietly. She started back up the road.

"Kat?" Kirk asked.

"Where's she going?" Randy asked.

Katherine was about halfway up the hill when she could more clearly see the light source. It was coming from a window in the attic floor of the west tower. It glowed softly and made shadows dance about the room. *What in the hell?*

AUGUSTINE PIERCE

Reaching the front doors, she found inside was completely dark, which meant only the west tower's attic was illuminated. She took out her flashlight and clicked it on. She ran across the entryway, into the left hallway, all the way to the base of the west tower.

She opened the tower's doors and found a small room with a spiral staircase. The flickering light from above spilled down the stairs, casting a faintly warm glow.

Under this glow, she noticed another shining angular pattern on the other side of the room. Like the one on the wall behind the entryway staircase, this one was also based on an equilateral triangle. Only this one had its left corner and circle missing, and had the addition of a V with a circle at its point sticking out of the triangle's bottom side.

"Almost like the one in the entryway." Remembering the reason she'd come back here, she raced up the spiral staircase of all four stories and found the window that she'd seen outside.

Directly beneath it stood a freshly lit candle. As she approached it, she felt a tingle run down her spine. "That's not possible," she told the attic. "None of us were up here." She thought about that. "Unless Shane came and set this up just to mess with me. But when? He was working with the rest of them the whole time."

THE HAUNTING OF BLACKSTONE MANSION

She was about to snuff out the candle when she remembered. "The light was turning." She faced the center of the attic and lifted her flashlight. At the upper edge of the light's beam, she saw a metallic sheen. She looked up. The cake stand she'd found during her first visit had been hung with a length of string by its base from a rafter in the ceiling. She gasped. "Oh my God. That was in the... in the kitchen. Got painfully cold. I tossed it or..."

She heard the tiniest sound. It resembled a mouse's squeak, but it lasted longer and was much deeper. She froze and listened. It was coming from under her. In front of her. From beyond the wall. The longer she listened, the more the squeak turned into a sort of whine, like the distant echo of a child throwing a tantrum.

She instinctively pointed her light at the top of the spiral staircase. Her mind was searching for the source of the sound, but she saw nothing that could be making it.

The sound grew louder and closer. Now it resembled a wail, like a woman crying at some profound heartbreak. *Sounds like when I first realized...*

Now she heard it directly in front of her, as if it were being amplified straight through the wall. Her eyes fixed on a point in the wall at her eye level.

An oily darkness oozed onto the surface, displacing the reflected rotating glow of the cake stand like a breath would blow the dust off the cover of an old book. The darkness stretched until it was only a few inches shorter than Katherine. It spread out until it settled into a humanoid shape with areas for a head, neck, shoulders, arms, and torso.

A shadow in a shadow! Katherine's mind screamed at her.

The darkness drifted along the wall's surface until it was only a few inches from her left. The right-hand area rose up the wall. A white spot appeared. It scratched against the wall's surface like an insect's claws pressing into the membrane of its egg sac.

A bony finger shot through the wall! Bits of rotting flesh and sinew still clung to it. Drops fell from it as if it had been left out in a rainstorm. It curled as if struggling to catch hold of an unseen edge.

The rest of the skeletal hand followed. Then the left one sprang forth, its bones twisting, stretching, and *crackling*. More bones emerged. Arms. Kneecaps. Shin bones. Ribs. The triangular ridge of a nasal cavity.

A grotesque, rotting corpse stepped out of the wall shadow. Ropes of soaked, matted hair swayed from the sides of the skull. A massive fracture cut from the top left of its forehead across to just below its right eye socket. A pulsing, chunky, black glob hung suspended from fleshy strands attached to its pubic bones and rib cage.

Katherine could not move. She could not think. She could not do anything but stare in terrified amazement at the nightmarish specter before her.

The skull tipped back. Dull sanguine pinpoints appeared at the very centers of its eye sockets. The hue instantly inflamed into copper and then intense, burning ember. The skull thrust forward. The jawbone dropped open. A wailing shriek like nothing Katherine had ever heard before exploded all around her. A freezing chill sucked out all of the heat from the room. A stench worse than anything she'd ever smelled shot up her nostrils and down her throat. The very floor and walls shook with fury.

Katherine's whole body released, every last muscle. She spewed forth all the breath her lungs contained into the loudest, most ear-shattering scream her diaphragm could squeeze out.

14

"Kat!" Kirk exclaimed.

Katherine's eyes darted over to him, but she said nothing.

"You okay?" he asked.

She looked straight ahead, fully expecting that horrible shrieking corpse to still be standing there.

There was nothing.

The space in front of her, along with the surface of the wall, was empty. The only reminder of what had just happened was the still-dangling cake stand and the flickering candlelight.

"I…" She had no idea what to say.

"You look like you've just seen a g—" he started.

She raised her hand. She couldn't let him say it. Keeping her eyes trained on the space before her, she ordered, "Get me outta here."

"Yeah. Of course. We're ready—"

"Now."

"Yeah." He held out his hand.

She stared at it as if it weren't real, as if it were just as fleeting as her encounter with the... with the... Finally, she wrapped her fingers around his hand and gripped tightly.

"That's it. You're okay." He looked up at the twisting cake stand. "What's *that* doing up there?"

"Now! Kirk!"

He nodded and walked her to the spiral staircase.

She looked back at the candle, at the cake stand. Her mind swam with the possibilities, none of which she allowed herself to fully consider. *Did she bring it up—? Did she light the—Has she been here the whole—Who is she?*

"One step at a time," Kirk said.

Katherine finally registered the sound of his voice and recognized that he was easing her down the stairs one step at a time. "Need to get outta here."

"We are. We're getting out."

Not frickin' fast enough! Her feet hammered down those stairs. She started skipping two, three at a time.

"Kat, be careful! Don't wanna fall."

She hardly listened to him as she raced down. The only thing that stopped her was that she ran out of stairs to descend. Her eyes searched eagerly for an exit. She found doors. She was about to leap for them when she felt a hand on her shoulder. She screamed.

AUGUSTINE PIERCE

"Whoa! Just me!" he tried to reassure her.

"Out."

"I know." He opened the right door and held it for her.

She emerged into the west-east hallway. She could not get to the entryway fast enough.

"Hold on, hold on." He caught up to her and kept stride right next to her. "Careful here."

They ran across the entryway, and out the doors.

Thank God, she thought on seeing the pitch black of the woods looming over the road down to the gate. She didn't dare look back up at that attic to see if the candle was still lit. For all she knew, the corpse had returned and was waiting to fix its glowing eye sockets on her again.

"Almost there," Kirk said as they practically ran down the hill.

Right outside the gate, the guys were waiting, clearly very ready to go.

"What was that all about?" Shane asked.

Kirk's tone was surgically cold. "Shane?"

Shane nodded and sheepishly backed away.

Kirk opened the gate for Katherine. "There you go. Step on through."

Katherine passed through, walked a few feet, but stopped in the middle of the road.

Randy asked Kirk quietly, "Everything good?"

"Just give her a sec."

THE HAUNTING OF BLACKSTONE MANSION

"What happened up there?" Dennis asked.

"I don't know, but..." Kirk took a few steps toward Katherine. "Kat? You okay to drive?"

Katherine didn't look at him. She could feel tears streaming down her cheeks. "Just get me outta here."

"Why don't you guys go ahead?" Kirk asked the others. "Let's meet at her place."

"We gettin' paid or what?" Shane asked.

"Jesus, Shane! I'll compensate you for your frickin' time, just please, help me out here."

Katherine heard three pairs of feet shuffle off. She then heard doors close and engines start.

"Kat?" Kirk asked. "If it's okay with you, I'm gonna drive you back."

Katherine nodded and finally looked up at him. Even in the darkness, she could see his face was full of concern. "Yeah."

"I'm gonna need your keys. Can you give me your keys?"

She nodded. She tried to reach into her pocket, but her fingers were shaking so much, she couldn't quite make them go in.

He took her hand. She shuddered even at that level of unexpected touch.

"It's all right," he said. "I'm gonna reach into your pocket now. Is that all right?"

She nodded.

"I'm reaching into your pocket," he said.

AUGUSTINE PIERCE

She felt the warmth of his fingers through the cloth. Under normal circumstances, she would have wanted him to use that hand to tear her pants off, bend her over the back of her car, and... Right now, though, all she wanted was to be as far away from the mansion as possible.

She felt his fingers poke around, then curl around her keys. His fingers lifted carefully out of her pocket, and she heard the clink of the keys glancing each other.

"I'm gonna walk you to the passenger side and let you in," he said.

She felt his warm grip around her arm. She relaxed as he gently tugged her along. She heard the door open. She reached out, found the seat, and climbed in as awkwardly as a toddler who was going on her first car ride.

She felt the seat belt stretch over her and tighten with a click. She heard her door close. Footsteps walked around the front of her car and stopped at the driver's side. She heard that door open, another seat belt stretch and click, then the door close.

The engine roared to life. The sudden loud sound made her shudder all over again. Tires ground along pavement. She raised her eyes to the windshield. To her absolute delight, she saw headlight beams illuminate a road stretching out ever before her, and dark, looming trees flying by. She looked back to see that awful black brick wall vanish into the darkness. *I never have to go back.*

"So, you wanna tell me what happened? Before I found you?"

How on earth do I even begin? She said nothing.

"That's cool. I'll just drive us back. You just chill, relax."

But she couldn't relax. She could barely wrap her mind around what had just happened. *Did it happen? Did that* actually *happen? Or did I eat some bad jerky? Did Shane sprinkle some ayahuasca dust on my sandwich when I wasn't looking just to screw with me?* Either of those possibilities was better than what she was coming to terms with had actually happened.

She heard a rhythm tapping on the steering wheel. Each tap felt like a cymbal crashing into her ears. "Could you, uh...?"

"Right. Sorry." The tapping ceased.

She continued to watch the road come at them and the trees stream by. She decided to count the trees. *One, two, three, crap, okay, missed that one, start over.* They were racing by too quickly for her to count. *One, two, three...* She'd started over ten times when she saw the lights of Blackstone's buildings. She must have visually perked up because he clearly noticed.

"That's right. Almost home."

Soon they passed by the town square, and before she knew it, they'd parked in front of her house.

He turned off the engine and unstrapped his seat belt. "Gimme one sec to square things with the guys and I'll be right back."

"I'll totally pay 'em. I just..."

"Don't worry about that right now. I'll take care of it."

She nodded.

His door opened and closed. She heard his footsteps walk a little then stop. She heard his voice, though not completely clearly. Something about "take care of her" and "go ahead and go home."

She heard Randy ask, "What do we do with all the stuff?"

She heard Dennis ask, "What about your truck?"

There was a pause before Kirk answered. "Go ahead and take it home, cover it up with a tarp or something so nobody sees. I'll text you. Um, I'll pick my truck up later."

"I don't understand what the hell is—" Shane said.

"Don't wanna help me out, fine, we'll unload your truck and you can go."

"No, no. I just... I wanna make sure she's okay."

"Sure you do," Dennis said.

"Blow it out your ass."

"All right, I'll text you guys," Kirk said.

THE HAUNTING OF BLACKSTONE MANSION

Katherine heard murmurs of agreement followed by receding footsteps, closing doors, engines starting up, and finally, her driver's side door open.

Kirk got in and closed the door. "All good for now. Want me to walk you to your door?"

"Sean's."

"Sorry?"

"Sean's Bar and Grill." She faced him. "I need a goddamn drink."

Katherine knocked back the latest shot. She didn't know how many she'd had, but she'd rather have been hospitalized for alcohol poisoning than ever again have to think about what she'd seen tonight.

She slammed the glass on the bar. "Hit me again."

"Uh..." the bartender, Nick, uttered, then paused.

Kirk held up an index finger for Nick to give them a second. Nick nodded and checked in on other customers.

Katherine whined after Nick. "You scared away my shot dispenser!"

"Kat," Kirk said.

She bent over the bar and pleaded longingly to Nick's back. "Come back, shot dispenser."

"Kat?" Kirk asked.

She sat up, swiped her empty shot glass, held it over her mouth, flipped it over, and shook vigorously in an attempt to shake out any remaining drops. She got two. "Yes!" She slammed the glass on the bar again.

He took her tiny moment of regrouping her thoughts to collect her glass and set it far out of her reach.

"You took my glass, you meanie poop-head!" she whined.

"Kat, look at me," he pleaded.

She focused on him for a few seconds.

"What happened tonight? You were fine earlier, excited about selling all those"—he looked around in case someone was listening—"pieces, then this." He indicated her empty shot glass.

She heaved a huge sigh, drooped her head back, inhaled deeply, and cackled a little. "Oh my God. Is that Bobby?" She was referring to the man who had hit on her the other night.

Sure enough, Bobby was among friends by the pool tables. He looked embarrassed at having been pointed out.

She waved. "Hey, Bobby!"

Bobby turned away from her gaze, focusing on his friends.

"Who's Bobby?" Kirk asked.

Katherine lifted her head. "What's the point?"

THE HAUNTING OF BLACKSTONE MANSION

"What do you mean what's the point?"

She finally faced him and looked like she was going to stay focused. "Dean doesn't believe me, and he's been my best friend since kindergarten, and that was only about the shadow. This... And you don't even know me!"

"It doesn't matter how well I know you. I'm concerned."

"Really? Oh, you're so sweet." Tears rolled down her cheeks.

He scooped up a napkin and handed it to her.

She wiped her eyes, balled up the napkin, and tossed it. "What am I doing? I don't drink like this. Not for *years*. Oh, you don't have to stay. I know this has nothing to do with you. Thanks for driving me over here." She scooted on her stool with the intention to stand, but gravity had other ideas.

He stuck his arm behind her so she wouldn't fall and eased her back onto her seat. "I'm not goin' anywhere."

She grinned like a teenage boy who knew he was about to get laid. "Oh, I know what you're doing. You think you're gonna get lucky." She swooped her index finger around like a toy airplane and landed it on his nose.

He gently moved her finger aside, placed her hand on the bar, and immediately removed his hand. "Kat?"

"Yes, Kirk," she said very formally, her suggestion of his desire for her having already completely slipped her mind.

"What happened?"

She shut her eyes for a second and sighed again. "You asked for it. You're gonna think I'm so crazy." She proceeded to tell him her adventures of the past few days, including every last detail, from the instantly freezing cake stand right up until that banshee of a dripping, rotting corpse.

His expression remained serious. There wasn't even a hint of a grin on his lips. "I don't think you're crazy."

"You don't?"

"Not at all. Crazy people don't doubt themselves."

"So what do you think—?"

"I don't know, but not only do I not think you're crazy, I'm sure you saw something."

"Yes! Thank you! I saw a *ton* of something! But I don't know what to do about it."

"You can look up the history of the house, see if there were ever any cold cases related to it. You can start tomorrow. As soon as you get up."

"Oh crap! Friday! Miles, Aleeyah, and Chase are gonna be there! Crap! The guns and furniture! They're with the guys!"

"I can get the stuff dropped off. Don't worry about that."

"You can? Oh, thank God! But the buyers. I don't know how I'm gonna face them after... after what I..." She seized Kirk's hands. "Will you stay with me? Tonight? It's not a hit-on."

He nodded. "I understand."

"I just can't be alone."

"Happy to. Why don't we get you outta here?"

She reached into her purse. "Crap, I gotta pay for all these."

He placed his hand on hers digging for money. "Don't worry about it. Seriously. I'll take care of the tab. Let's get you home."

"Really?" Tears trickled down her cheeks again.

He nodded emphatically. "Really."

Katherine stumbled up the path to her front door. She would have fallen flat on her face but for her arm around Kirk's tall, muscular, steadying body.

When they reached the door, she panicked. "Oh crap!"

"What?"

"Where're my keys?"

"Right here." He took them out of his pocket and jingled them.

"What are *you* doing with my keys?"

"I drove you home."

"Right. Sorry." She laughed.

He kept her upright as he unlocked the front door and let them in. He then walked her to the couch and sat her down before going back and closing the door. "Where's your bedroom?"

She pointed up.

"All right, let's get you up there." He reached down and pulled her to her feet.

"You're strong!"

"Somewhat."

"No, you're *really* strong!"

With his help, she stumbled up the stairs, down the hall, and into her bedroom. She was about to simply drop into bed, when she felt his hand on her shoulder.

"No, no," he said. "Let's get you ready."

The next thing she knew, her arms were lifting up and her jacket was slipping off. "You just wanna undress me."

"I do"—he poked his head into her view—"but not for that." He turned her ninety degrees toward him. Her jacket was slung over his arm. He pointed to her crotch. "Can you get that or do you need help?"

"My lady part?"

He looked like he was struggling to maintain patience. "No, Katherine, your button and zipper."

"Oh, we're being formal now." She saw that he wasn't amused by her comment. "I can get it." She undid her pants and let them drop. They only fell a little. "Can you...?"

He did his best to avert his eyes from her legs, but couldn't help looking a little. "I'm gonna pull. Can you step out?"

"Yeah."

He got her out of her jeans and draped them over his arm next to her jacket. "I'm gonna hang these up—"

"One more thing."

"What's that?"

She pointed to her butt and sighed. "I was... freaked out."

He nodded. "Happens to the best of us."

"Uh-huh? Have you ever?"

"Where's your clean underwear?"

She pointed to a drawer.

He walked over, opened it, then paused. "How about this?" He faced her. "I'm gonna step out, you take off your undies, put on a fresh pair, knock on the door, I'll come back in, tuck you in?"

"I think I should, uh..." She pointed down the hall.

"Okay." He sounded like he was losing track of what was going on.

She walked down the hall to the bathroom, went in, and closed the door. Inside, she took off her underwear, did *not* take a look at them, cleaned herself off with wads of toilet paper, flushed that down, then knocked on the door.

"I'm not looking," he said through the door. "Just gonna pass you a fresh pair."

She grinned wide. "You touched my underwear?"

"Yeah. I'm sorry. I..."

"Kirk, it's okay."

"All right."

"Kirk?"

"Yeah?"

"Thanks for doing all this. I know you didn't have to."

"It's fine, Kat. Just wanna make sure you're good."

"Ready."

He opened the door, and without looking in her direction passed her a fresh pair of underwear.

She took them and closed the door. "Thanks."

"Yeah."

She slid on the fresh pair, looked down at the soiled ones, decided she'd deal with that later, and opened the door.

"Ready for bed?" he asked.

"After you."

He walked her back into the bedroom, stood her next to the bed while he peeled back the blankets, then eased her onto the bed.

THE HAUNTING OF BLACKSTONE MANSION

She slid under the blankets, and as he covered her up, she took the opportunity to wrap her arms around his neck and whisper to him, "I wanna sleep with you so bad. I want you inside me. I want—"

He patiently lifted her arms from around his neck and placed them at her sides. "You're drunk."

"I'm sobering."

"Good night." He stood up straight. "Need anything, I'll be right downstairs." He walked out of the room.

"Kirk?"

He stopped and turned around. "Yeah?"

"I'm really sorry, but I don't wanna be alone."

"Katherine, you're drunk. You may not think you are, but—"

"No, I don't mean sex. Just stay in here, please."

He nodded. "Okay."

"You can steal the cushions and pillows from the couch. I think there's another set of sheets in a closet."

"I'll find it."

"Thanks, Kirk."

"Good night, Katherine."

She tried to stay awake long enough to make sure that he'd return with pillows and blankets and make himself a makeshift bed next to hers and wait while she fell asleep, but before she knew it, her eyes closed and she passed out.

15

Katherine leaned over Kirk and his makeshift bed. "I owe you a huge apology."

It was very early the next morning, and she'd woken up only about a minute ago.

"Sorry?"

"Last night."

"It's fine."

"No. I know I said and did some things that, if our genders were reversed, would've been considered harassment, and I apologize."

"I pardon you."

"Great. What did I say and do?"

"Not much. Had some shots. Forgot I had your keys. That sort of thing."

"Did I tell you about mansion stuff?"

He nodded.

"And you still don't think I'm crazy?" she asked.

"No. I'd actually suggested you look into it."

"Yeah. Um, did I come on to you?"

He shrugged. "Not really."

"Oh my God. I totally came on to you." She sat up and fell back against the wall.

"It wasn't that bad."

"I'm so embarrassed. What did I say?"

"I mean, it was kind of mumbled."

"You're a terrible liar. I told you I wanted to sleep with you. I told you I wanted you inside me! God..."

"Kat, it's really okay. You were drunk."

"You must think I'm the biggest..."

He sat up. "How about this? How about I go downstairs and make us some breakfast while you get dressed? Forget all about last night. Or about all the parts that you wanna forget."

She nodded. "Sounds great."

He stood up and gathered his makeshift bed things. "See you downstairs." He walked out.

The second he was out of sight, she buried her face in her pillow and whined good and hard. "Kat, what is wrong with you?"

Finally fully dressed, she descended the stairs to the cheerful, whistling, cooking Kirk. Whatever it was that he'd thrown together, smelled amazing. "What *is* that?"

"Scrambled eggs with a little bit of mustard. I figured scrambled eggs never hurt anybody. So far as we know."

"Might've stolen the Limbergh baby." She sat at the kitchen table.

"Sorry?"

"You said scrambled eggs never hurt anybody. I was suggesting how they might've."

He laughed. "That's funny."

"Nah, if you gotta explain it..."

He shrugged. "I'm slow." He dished her up a plate, made a plate for himself, and joined her at the table. "After we're done, I'm gonna call the guys, get the firearms and furniture over here as quick as we can. Get one of them to drive me up to the mansion so I can get my truck, then come back with that stuff. I'm no antiques expert, but is this really the best place to put everything?"

"Either that or I rent a chilly, dusty storage space three towns away."

"I'll tell 'em to drop it off here."

She suddenly remembered. "And I've gotta pay you guys."

"Technically me."

"What do you mean?"

"I paid them last night."

"When?"

"Right before Sean's."

"How'd you know I'd be out of it?"

"I didn't. Always be prepared."

"You're a Boy Scout too?"

"Yes, was, but their motto's only 'be prepared.'"

"Well, then I gotta pay you."

THE HAUNTING OF BLACKSTONE MANSION

"Take your time."

"No, no. You've been more than patient. While you're on the phone with them, I'll go to the ATM. That way, by the time they get here, I'll have the cash."

"Sounds like a plan."

They ate their breakfast in silence. *I can't believe I so explicitly threw myself at him!* She stood. "I'm gonna..." She pointed upstairs.

"Yeah, of course. I'll clean up here and call the guys."

"Great." She went upstairs and threw her clothes on. When she came back down, she saw he was already on the phone, so she smiled, and left.

At the ATM, she felt a tiny bit nervous at taking out so much cash. She looked over her shoulder several times to make sure no one was approaching. *After what I saw last night, a mugger would be a welcome sight.*

She returned to the house with the cash, placed it on the kitchen table, and declared, "All there."

"Great!" He pocketed it. "The guys should be here in about twenty."

"Just the right amount of time to do nothing."

"Isn't it, though?"

"Coffee?"

"Sure."

She brewed them each a mug, and they sat on the couch and engaged in awkward chitchat while they waited for the others.

"This is good," he said.

"Yeah?"

"Yeah."

"I got it at that small place down the street."

"Don't think I know that one."

"You know, the place down the street."

"Oh right! Down *the* street!"

They both laughed at their silly, junior high banter.

A knock at the door interrupted the awkwardness.

"You kids at home?" Randy asked.

Katherine got up and let him, Dennis, and Shane in.

"How we all doin'?" Dennis asked very suggestively.

"We're good," Kirk said flatly.

"Where you want us to dump all the stuff?" Shane asked.

"Wherever you can fit it in here." Katherine gestured to the living room.

"In *here* here?" Shane asked.

"Yeah."

"Well, you'll pardon my impudence, ma'am, but shouldn't it all go into a museum? I thought that's what folks did with antiques."

THE HAUNTING OF BLACKSTONE MANSION

"No, they keep 'em to show off to their rich friends," Randy said.

"No, they only keep their faves, toss the junk into museums," Dennis said.

You're not far off, Dennis. "Gotta sell 'em first," Katherine said as if she'd done so a thousand times already.

"Hey, your call," Shane said.

Kirk set his mug down on the coffee table near the jewelry box. "Why don't we go ahead and take care of it?"

"I guess I'll wait upstairs," Katherine said. "Someone come get me when you guys are done?"

The guys all murmured their agreement.

With that, she finished her coffee, placed the mug in the sink, and retreated upstairs.

---

*G*hosts *are real.* Katherine sat on her bed contemplating that idea with her open laptop next to her, for what felt like several minutes. Even after seeing what she'd seen, she still couldn't wrap her head around it. *And what does it mean? Did I step on its grave? Wait. It had that gross long hair. Was it a she? Okay, obviously, I didn't step on her grave since I was in the attic.* "Does she want something from me? How could she? I have no connection to the family." *Unless* *she wants my help.* "Maybe it wasn't me she was angry at. Maybe she just wanted to get my attention."

She lay next to her laptop. "So, Miss Shrieky McRedeyes, who are you?" She googled the Blackstone family and easily found names and pictures of each of them as well as family portraits. "Vernon, Gloria, Reginald, and Marcus." There weren't any images of anything that looked like a rotting corpse. "If you were a servant, they're not gonna include you in any family portraits. Were you a cousin?" She did another search for any Blackstone family reunions. She came up with only two pictures. There were a few women among the groups. She looked up, past the laptop. "What am I thinking? I saw a… a corpse. She could've been Gloria. Could've been any of these women." Her eyes dropped back down to the laptop. "What was the social media of their day? What did the wealthy do in the twenties? Vernon hunted, but it's unlikely he would've gone with any women. Gloria was most likely involved in society events, charities. Let's see what she was up to." Sure enough, she found Gloria all over charities, balls, and other high-society events. There were headlines about the Rose Festival banquet, the opening of the Blackstone Family wing at the Portland Art Museum in downtown, but nothing brought her any closer to last night's specter.

THE HAUNTING OF BLACKSTONE MANSION

Katherine sat up. "She was in the mansion. Assuming she's been trapped there, maybe she also died there. If she died there, and she was a relative, she was most likely Gloria. If she wasn't a relative, she could've been a servant, but if she wasn't, she had to have been invited to the mansion. Let's assume she was Gloria. Had that huge friggin' crack in her skull." She googled Gloria Blackstone cause of death, finding an obituary from 1920. "Natural causes? A guillotine to the forehead isn't frickin' natural. Maybe not Gloria, then. Maybe a servant. If her death was an accident, would she be hanging around? Do ghosts resent accidents?" *God, listen to me. This is so ridiculous.* "But it happened, Kat."

She stood up from her bed and paced. "If she was a servant and she was murdered at the mansion, how would I find out? Could there've been an investigation?"

She sat down on the bed again and started frantically typing. As soon as one tab started to load results, she opened another. She wanted as many possibilities as she could have at once while the ideas were fresh. She looked up Blackstone mansion servant investigation, Blackstone mansion murder investigation, Blackstone family murder investigation, and Blackstone family missing servant.

Nothing.

"No to servants, even murdered or missing. If she wasn't a servant, who the hell was she?"

"Kat?" Kirk asked from the hall. In another second, he was at her bedroom doorway.

"Hey." she hadn't yet looked up at him as she was still distracted with her lack of search results.

"We're good to go."

She finally looked up from her laptop. "I'm sorry, what?"

"We're done down here."

"Oh great! Uh, okay, thanks." She stood and followed him downstairs.

Kirk and his guys had squeezed the furniture into the center of the living room like *Tetris* blocks. The firearms, they'd stacked here and there and everywhere within every square foot available, without damaging any pieces. They'd miraculously managed to maintain a clear line from the stairs to the front door and the door to the kitchen.

"Wow, can't believe you got it all in," Katherine said.

"Took some squeezin', but yeah," Dennis said.

"I guess that's it." *Don't leave. Don't leave me here. What if corpse lady comes back or who knows who else?* "I'll, uh, walk you guys out."

Dennis and Shane threw a glance at the front door and gawked at her. It wasn't exactly that far to go to be walked out.

THE HAUNTING OF BLACKSTONE MANSION

Katherine opened the front door for them. As each of Kirk's guys left, she thanked them.

"Thanks for the job," Kirk said.

"Thanks for, uh, tucking me in," Katherine said.

"Anytime." He stepped out.

"Kirk?"

"Yeah?"

"Do you know anything about the Blackstone family, like, any unsolved mysteries? Missing persons? Murders?"

"No, why?"

"Nothing huge, I just thought… Nothing. Thanks."

He smiled. "Gimme a ring if you need anything."

"I will. Bye."

He walked a few feet to his truck, then turned around. "You should ask Jordan."

"What?"

"About any family skeletons in the closet. Ask him when you give him the check."

She nodded. "Good idea."

"Let me know how it goes." He got in his truck.

I will.

Katherine had been pacing for a few minutes in the living room, pondering Blackstone family history, the sale of the items currently surrounding her, and a good excuse to reach out to Kirk, when she heard the doorbell ring. *Didn't even think there was a doorbell!* "One second!"

She negotiated her way past the rifles and sofas to the front door. Opening it, she found Drew carrying a covered baking dish. "Drew! Good morning."

"'Morning, Kat. I know it's a bit odd for me to show up on a Thursday morning, but my wife made you a batch of that peach cobbler I told you about, so I thought I'd bring it by."

"Wow, great, that's so kind of her." She did her damnedest to keep the door shut as much as possible while doing her best to not make it look obvious. She could tell, though, that he was eager to come in. *Yeah, I don't think so, Drew.*

He passed her the cobbler. "You can keep the dish. We got plenty." He chuckled.

She was so distracted by not letting him in that she hadn't even registered what he'd said. "The dish?"

He nodded at the dish.

"Right. Oh my God. Thank your wife for me. I haven't had a chance to pick up any of my own."

"Busy moving in?"

Please just go, Drew. "Uh, yeah, related, you know, business stuff."

"I don't think I ever asked, what business are you in?"

THE HAUNTING OF BLACKSTONE MANSION

She really hoped that her answer would bore him as it bored almost all men. "Antiques."

His face lit right up. "My wife loves antiquing! She drags me out to the coast at least once a month to look at old junk."

"She sounds quite talented." *What the hell does that mean?*

"I'll put you two in touch. I bet you have a lot in common."

I deal in very rare collectors' items to the ultra-rich, Drew, not the occasional seventies' lawn chair. "I bet we do."

He took out his phone. "Here. I'll give you her number."

"Oh, I don't have my phone on me. Left it upstairs."

"I can wait." His tone was polite, but the corners of his mouth were falling from a smile to impatience.

Just get it over with and get him on his way. "Be right back." She closed the door, set the cobbler on the kitchen table, and started down the path to the stairs, when she heard the door creak. *Crap.*

Sure enough, Drew had let himself in. And his eyes were so wide they looked like they might bulge straight out of his head. "What in the hell is this?"

"Drew, I can explain—"

"That's Mr. Barrister to you, Ms. Norrington."

"Mr. Barrister, I can explain."

"I thought I was very clear."

"Yes, you were."

"The first floor is my *father's* space."

"Yes, I recall."

"It doesn't seem you do because there's currently a gigantic pile of... What is all this?"

"These are antiques which I am going to sell tomorrow to very eager buyers. The only reason I put them here is I needed a safe place where I could keep my eye on them, and since I don't have a storefront yet..."

He squatted next to the nearest rifle and reached out to pick it up.

"Please don't touch that," she said.

He completely ignored her and lifted up the gun's business end for a second. "Are these guns, Ms. Norrington?"

"They are antique firearms, yes."

He glared up at her. "You're trafficking stolen arms out of my daddy's house?"

"They're not stolen!"

He stood up straight and crossed his arms. "Did you purchase them?"

"I have permission from the owner!"

"Did you get that in writing, Ms. Norrington?"

"Drew—"

"Mr. Barrister."

"They will be out of your father's space—"

"His *home*."

"They'll be out of here by tomorrow morning."

"I'm afraid, Ms. Norrington, that's not good enough."

"What do you mean?"

He nodded at the jewelry box. "My wife's is a crappy trinket we got her at Target. I bet I'd earn myself a whole month's worth of BJs if I brought that pretty thing home."

Katherine winced. *Gonna take me forever to get that image outta my head!* "You're kidding. The box alone is worth over, like, twenty grand."

His eyebrows lifted right up. "I'd say that's about settled." He moved to go and collect the jewelry box.

She went after him and grabbed his arm. "No, it's part of the sale! You can't just—"

He flicked her hand off, turned around, and got in her face. His nostrils flared. His eyes blazed. "I loved my daddy, Ms. Norrington! Now, maybe you don't know what it's like to lose someone so close to you, but it tore me in half! I promised myself I would maintain his house as best I could. Now, either you clear out of it and take all your crap with you, or I'm calling the police!"

"Actually, Drew, I know exactly what that's like and I absolutely empathize. I was ripped in two weeks ago, and I frankly don't know how I'm gonna put myself back together, but moving here, to Oregon's rural peace and quiet, and setting myself up at least for a little while with this sale, was all gonna be part of it. Now, please, I will have this stuff out of your father's house by tomorrow."

He seemed to have calmed at least a tiny bit, but then he bent over, swiped the first item he could wrap his fingers around, a pristine Winchester rifle, shoved her aside, and stormed out.

"What are you doing?" She ran after him.

"Helpin' you"—he raised the rifle above his head and tossed it as hard as he could at the stone path from the front door—"out!"

Bam! The rifle fired.

He stumbled back and nearly fell into the front door. "They're loaded?!" He swung around to face her and looked like he was going to punch her in the jaw, but he restrained himself.

"I didn't know! That's why they have to be handled carefully!"

"If I see you or any of your crap in here in one hour, I'm calling the police!"

"How am I supposed to move all of this out in an hour?"

He stomped off to his car. "Figure it out, Ms. Norrington!"

THE HAUNTING OF BLACKSTONE MANSION

Katherine frantically picked up as many rifles as she could hold and carried them out to the back of her car. She set them on the ground and opened the trunk.

The amount of space was pitiful. She could tell instantly that the width alone was insufficient to hold a single rifle. *Pistols'll go in there*. She closed the trunk and opened the back driver's side door. There was precious little space. She picked up one of the rifles and slid it in back. It fit, but she could tell not many more would, and it would hardly be safe to stack them up back there. If even one was loaded and she hit a bump in the road... "It's ten minutes' drive to that motel, ten minutes back, so if I can grab at least five of these... The furniture. There's no way I can fit it in this car." She paused and took a breath to center. "If I don't move anything, he'll just think I'm being an obstinate bitch. But there's no way I can move even half of it." *Crap. Screw it. Gotta try.*

She put the rest of the rifles that were resting on the ground into the back seat, then ran back into the house to grab a few more.

By the time she was heading out to the motel, she had a trunk full of pistols and a back seat packed with rifles. She hoped to hell no cops took notice of any of it while she was on the road.

She arrived at the motel in about eight minutes, but doubted that those extra two minutes she'd saved would make much of a difference. She checked in as quickly as she could, though the clerk seemed to take his sweet time running her card.

She moved the car to directly in front of her room, ran to her motel room door, and opened it wide. She ran back to her car, popped the trunk, scooped up as many pistols as she could carry, and brought them inside. She repeated the process till her car was empty of firearms. She locked the room and sped back to her soon-to-be vacated house, as quickly as she could.

Pulling up to the house, she saw a sheriff's car already parked in front alongside Drew's car. Drew and the sheriff were standing in the middle of the front yard, the sheriff patiently listening to Drew's tirade. She checked the time. Twenty-eight minutes had passed since Drew had taken off.

"That's not even a half hour!" she groaned. She jumped out of her car and ran straight up to Drew. "You said an hour!"

The sheriff got between her and Drew. "Let's try to stay calm, ma'am."

"You got that in writing?" Drew asked.

"Mr. Barrister, I am sorry for placing antiques on your late-father's floor, but this is completely ridiculous!" she exclaimed.

THE HAUNTING OF BLACKSTONE MANSION

"You see, Officer? Utterly hysterical! And she admits it! She dumped the antiques! My father's floor!" Drew shouted.

"Mr. Barrister, please let me handle this." The sheriff turned his attention to Katherine. "Ma'am, is it true you're renting from Mr. Barrister?"

"Yes."

"And you have a signed contract to that effect?"

"I... We were gonna... He said he'd e-mail me something."

The sheriff grunted. "And did you agree not to use the first floor of the property?"

"Does he have *that* in writing?" She figured if Drew was going to be petty, she might as well toss a little back.

"It was a *verbal* agreement!" Drew shouted.

"Sir, please let me handle this," the sheriff reminded him. "Ma'am, do you have a license for these firearms?"

"I don't need one. They're antiques."

"Are they your property?"

"No, they're the property of a business associate." *Please don't ask about my agreement with Jordan.*

"Ask her if she can prove that!" Drew insisted.

"Sir?" the sheriff asked patiently. "And how are you related to this associate, ma'am?"

"I'm an antiques dealer. I'm gonna sell his antiques for a commission. Tomorrow."

The sheriff gestured for her to follow him. They walked a few yards away from Drew.

"Yeah, lock her up and throw away the key!" Drew shouted.

"Sir, I've warned you. Don't make me warn you again," the sheriff advised. "Ma'am," he spoke in a low tone, "as you can see, he's awful fired up. You got a place you can stay tonight?"

"I've already checked in at the motel down the road."

"I advise you to stay there one or two more nights, just till we can sort this whole thing out."

"What's there to sort out? I'm not in breach of any rental agreement."

"Ma'am, if Mr. Barrister insists, that'd mean you're technically squatting."

She sighed. "I have every right to keep those antiques."

"That is yet to be determined."

"What are you talking about? I have the owner's permission."

"Unfortunately, this might be an instance where Mr. Barrister is correct. Do you have proof that you have the owner's permission to hold his antiques?"

She sighed. "We have a verbal agreement."

"See? I told ya! Nothing in writing!" Drew cheered.

"Sir? One more disruptive outburst and I'm taking you in," the sheriff said. He turned back to Kather-

THE HAUNTING OF BLACKSTONE MANSION

ine. "You don't have anything in writing? Anything at all? Even a Post-it note or napkin?"

"Look, how about I call him and have him tell you?"

The sheriff nodded.

Katherine took out her phone and tapped Jordan's number.

He picked up immediately. "Kathy! Wasn't expecting to hear from you for another couple of days."

"Hey, Jordan. Uh, I've got a little situation here. I'm speaking with a very kind and patient sheriff—"

"Did you say 'sheriff'? What did you do, Kathy?"

"Nothing. I just need you to quickly do something for me."

"And what is that, exactly?"

"Could you please let this officer know that I do, in fact, have your permission to handle your family's antiques for the purpose of assessing and selling them?"

"Why would the kind sheriff need to know that?"

"There's been a misunderstanding out here, and the sheriff merely needs your confirmation that I am in lawful possession of your items."

There was a long pause. "Yeah, I'm afraid I can't do that."

Crap! Am I about to get arrested? "But, Jordan, that's what we agreed on."

213

"I remember hearing something about my not having to do any work at all. This kinda feels like work."

"Jordan, please, I just need you to—"

"Gotta go, Kath. Any more of these little inconveniences, especially from Johnny Law, and not only is our deal off, but my itchy fingers might end up calling my attorneys in regard to your tendency toward harassment."

Katherine couldn't believe her ears. How could this day get any worse?

"Bye-bye." Jordan hung up.

Katherine kept the phone by her mouth as if the conversation hadn't just ended. "I swear Jordan Blackstone and I have an arrangement."

The sheriff waved it off and smiled. "I can hold off on bustin' out the handcuffs."

She exhaled.

"But without proof of your contractual agreement with Mr. Blackstone, I am gonna have to confiscate the items in the house," he said. "Just to keep this all on the up-and-up."

"What?" she asked. "For how long?"

"Just till we can get Mr. Blackstone to confirm your relationship."

"No! I've got a sale tomorrow! There's no way they'll buy—I can't..." She didn't know what else to say or do.

"Ma'am, I'm very sorry, but—"

She held up her hands in surrender, then put her phone back in her pocket. "Please be careful with everything. They're antiques. And some may be loaded." She walked to her car.

"Are you arresting her?" Drew demanded. "Why aren't you arresting her?"

"Sir, if you could please…"

Katherine didn't hear the rest. She got in her car and drove back to the motel. *Great. There goes my deposit.*

16

Katherine woke to her phone's *buzz*. She lifted her head and stared at the device sitting all the way over, under the TV. She was still dressed in yesterday's clothes and she'd slept on top of the covers, having collapsed onto the bed once she'd arrived.

After the previous day's debacle with Drew, she'd spent the remainder of the day watching documentaries on non-firearm weaponry, eating snacks, and generally feeling sorry for herself until she'd passed out for the night.

Who the hell is it now? She got up and walked over to her phone. It was Aleeyah. "Oh no. I totally forgot to tell them I'm not there." She answered, "Aleeyah?"

"Hey! 'Morning! I didn't wake you up, did I?"

"No."

"I totally woke you up. Well, you should be up anyway since Miles and I and some other guy are here." She whispered, "I notice you didn't warn me about Miles."

THE HAUNTING OF BLACKSTONE MANSION

"Yeah, sorry, slipped my mind."

"Well, when are you going to be here? And... where are you?"

Katherine heard Miles's voice in the background. "Did she say where she is?"

"No. Miles, shut up," Aleeyah said. "So, Kat, where are you?"

"I'll be there in half an hour."

"Half an hour?" Aleeyah asked with complete incredulity.

Katherine hung up.

Katherine arrived at her recently vacated former house and found three luxury rentals parked along the front, with Miles, Aleeyah, and Chase standing together in the front yard.

Miles was handsome with short, dark hair and a long, black coat. Aleeyah was equally striking with professionally styled hair, a beautiful face, and a gray coat. Chase was shorter than Miles, with salon-styled hair, fashionable sunglasses, and a black jacket with no tie.

Katherine parked just beyond the house's property so if Drew were to suddenly show, he couldn't accuse her of trespassing.

She got out and gave her three visitors her brightest, shiniest smile. "Good morning, you guys!"

"'Morning!" Miles said.

"Look at you!" Aleeyah opened her arms wide to embrace Katherine.

"So, rural Oregon, huh, Katie?" Chase asked. "Very *Stand by Me.*"

Katherine hugged Aleeyah, then addressed them all. "Thank you all for coming here on such short notice. I don't think you'll be disappointed." She walked to her car, opened the back driver's side door, then the trunk.

"Why are they all wrapped up?" Aleeyah asked.

"Not much show space around here."

"Why do you have 'em in your car?" Chase asked.

"Um, it's a bit of a story."

"Is that all of them?" Mile asked. "I thought you said it was Mr. Blackstone's private collection."

"It's some of them, yes."

"Wasn't there a jewelry box with Mrs. Blackstone's prized necklace?" Aleeyah asked.

"Yeah, and what about all the furniture?" Chase asked.

You gotta tell 'em. "So, that's all with the police."

"Police?" Miles asked.

"Technically, sheriff."

"Oh my God, what happened?" Aleeyah asked.

"You been dealin' drugs, Katie?" Chase asked.

"Are you all right, darling? If you need any help, any help at all, I have the best attorneys in Manhattan."

"Fine and no on the drugs," Katherine said. "I wish I were. It's a really long story. Mix-up with my landlord. Or, former landlord. Point is, the police are holding the majority of the pieces till ownership is sorted out."

"I thought you had an arrangement with the owner," Miles said.

"I do. It's complicated."

"You're not sleeping with him?" Aleeyah asked.

"Not that kind of complicated."

"I mean, no judgment if you are, darling. Outside of, you know, the obvious ethical breach, conflict of interest, and all that."

"No, Leeyah, not sleeping with him."

"So how long are they holding the merchandise?" Miles asked.

"I don't know."

Chase chuckled sarcastically, turned partly away, and scoffed, "Can't believe I flew up here for this."

"Try across the pond, mate," Miles said.

"I'm really sorry, you guys," Katherine said. "I didn't mean for this to happen, and if you can stay for just a few days…"

"Days?" Miles asked.

"Eh, it's a write-off," Chase said. "I'll scour for other stuff in Portland."

Aleeyah dropped all of her previous warm and helpful pretense. "I do have a business to attend to, Katherine."

"So this is it?" Miles asked.

"Here"—Katherine nodded at the back seat—"and there." She pointed to the trunk.

"It's just, without the whole collection, plus the furniture from the room, full authentication from the owner... Well, they're nice pieces, but..."

Chase took a closer look at one of the Winchesters. "I'll take it all off your hands for seventy-five."

"Oh, you can fold that five ways and shove it," Katherine said.

"Eighty."

"Leeyah, I know you have a business to run, you gotta get back, and I respect that, but this was completely outta my control. If you can hang out just a couple of days, I'm sure we can do this the right way."

"Ninety."

"Why do you keep going up?" Miles asked.

"Movie props, dude. Studios, cosplayers, gun nuts. It is *ripe* down south, my friend."

"Perhaps I should consider an expansion."

"I don't know, darling," Aleeyah said. "How long did you say the police were going to be holding the rest?"

THE HAUNTING OF BLACKSTONE MANSION

"It won't be long," Katherine said.
"One double ostrich egg," Chase said.

K atherine sat in her firearm-free car with a shiny check for one hundred thousand dollars courtesy of Chase. She wanted to cry. Had she been able to sell the whole of Mr. Blackstone's gun room, her commission alone would have been bigger than this entire check. She would have been set up for years in Blackstone. With the commission from the sale of the entire contents of the house? Decades. *Well, maybe once I give Jordan his cut, he'll let me sell the rest.*

She got on her way to Portland. She wasn't about to deposit this much money in the ATM across the street from the town square and she didn't suspect any local banks would handle it particularly well either. She'd go to some shiny branch of some major bank up there. "It'll take around two business days to clear. I should at least prove to him that I did it." She'd show Jordan the check first, then go deposit it, then once the check cleared, come back with his share.

She was passing through Creek. She wanted to ring Kirk, wanted to see him, but she didn't have the time and didn't know what to say.

AUGUSTINE PIERCE

When she finally reached the Portland area, she was sick of the road, even though with her leisurely drive, it had only been about two hours. She just wanted to show Jordan the stupid check, have him officially sign off on the rest of the house, in writing, and get to it.

That woman. If Jordan let her represent his estate she'd be spending more time at the mansion. Would she see the rotting woman again? Maybe other ghosts? As much as she dreaded either encounter, or possibly others, she feared even more the possibility of trying to survive in Blackstone long-term on only her savings.

She arrived in Jordan's neighborhood. She marched right up to the Vista's door and rang his unit.

"Who is it?" Jordan asked.

"Hi, Jordan, it's Kat."

"That's weird. I thought I told you anything else and—"

"I have a check."

"You... you do?"

"Yep. Wanna let me up?"

"Uh, yeah. 'Course."

The front door buzzed. She went in. Riding the elevator, she was nervous. Would this amount be enough for him to let her sell the rest? She did brag

THE HAUNTING OF BLACKSTONE MANSION

to him that after this, he'd beg her to sell the rest. "Not much I can do now."

The elevator opened and she walked to his door. She rang the bell. She heard footsteps approach and held the check up at about his eye level. The door opened. She thrust it forward an inch for emphasis. "Feast on that."

It seemed like it took a long second for him to realize that a check was being held in front of his eyes. "Won't you come in?"

She lowered the check, entered, and made herself comfortable on the nearest end of a couch in the sunken area.

He closed the door. "Can I get you anything?"

"Jordan, I just showed you a check for quite a bit of money. Did you even wanna take a look at it?"

"Yeah, no, that's great, Kat."

At least he's stopped calling me Kathy.

He joined her on the end of the adjacent couch. "All right, what do we have?"

She passed him the check.

"Nice."

"That's it?"

"No, it's good. Not *quite* as much as I was hoping for, but, you know, yeah, good round number."

You've gotta be kidding me. "Okay, so..."

"Why's your name on it?"

"My associate conducted the transaction with me. Once I'm done here, I'll deposit it. In a few days, it'll clear—"

"A few days?"

"Standard for amounts this size."

"I gave you a week. That ends Sunday."

She was seriously starting to fantasize about grabbing the back of his head and slamming his face repeatedly into those red-hot glass shards in his firepit. "I agreed to catalog and auction one room. I did that."

"Could've sworn you said I'd be getting a check in a week."

"There's no way I could've guaranteed that, Jordan. I don't control bank policy."

"Oh, all right, fine. This counts." He handed the check back to her. "So, that check clears, you come back to me with a new one with my name on it?"

"Of course. Minus my commission."

"Excuse me?"

"Minus my commission."

"You said you were doing this at your expense."

"Yes, the labor, like, hiring guys to move all the stuff, providing moving supplies, supervising them. I did all that at my expense, but the sale, I get a commission. That's how I make my living." *Why am I explaining this to you?*

"Huh, I don't remember all that, but whatevs." He squinted his eyes suspiciously. "How much is your commission?"

"I'm fine with a standard ten percent."

"You're kidding me."

"No, I'm not."

"You're taking"—he held up the check so he could show off the number—"ten thousand dollars—"

"I *earned* ten thousand, yes."

"Of my money just for telling some goateed yokels where to stack a couple chairs?"

"It's also my experience, my expertise, my contacts."

"I could've just hired a U-Haul and driven a room full of junk down to a pawnshop."

"And made a ton less money."

He scoffed. "Ten percent. How about this? You either swap your name for mine, this full amount"—he shook the check for emphasis—"and I'll consider letting you rep my estate for the rest of the mansion, or you can slink off to your dinky apartment in that ass hair of a town and eagerly await word from my attorneys on multiple charges of trespassing, grand larceny, and trafficking of stolen goods?"

She shot to her feet and snatched the check. "Jordan, I earned my commission on this whether you're too stupid to realize it or not!"

AUGUSTINE PIERCE

His eyes snapped open and his jaw dropped. "Wow."

"And I would've thought you'd be just the tiniest, itsy bit *grateful* that due to my work so far, you're gonna be able to fund all your loud, gaudy, self-indulgent, toddler-tantrum"—she waved the check at the apartment—"Jordan-ness for that much longer!"

His mouth hung open, but he said nothing.

"But you know what? Fine! Once this check clears, I will send you one for an equal amount because if that means I'm no longer beholden to one of the most entitled, obnoxious, mean-spirited, insecure trust-fund babies to ever wrap his lips around a silver spoon, then fantastic!"

She folded the check neatly into quarters, shoved it into her pocket, and stomped out.

Katherine's time at the bank branch downtown was longer than she would have liked. The teller had to talk to the manager who talked to her who had to show ID, then contact information for Chase, then talk to the teller again, with several minutes between each step.

It gave her plenty of time to think. As much as she was furious with Jordan right now and frustrated at

THE HAUNTING OF BLACKSTONE MANSION

how their relationship had gone from one that she truly believed would bear plenty of fruit for both, to adversarial enough that he was now regularly threatening her with legal action, she couldn't stop thinking about... *that woman. Such rage.* Katherine obviously had no reason to ever return to Blackstone mansion, so she had no idea how she could have helped the rotting lady.

"So about two to three more business days, Ms. Norrington," the teller said.

"Thanks." Katherine exited.

Outside, she felt like she recognized the neighborhood more than she should. "Wait. Isn't the Blackstone wing of the art museum only a few blocks from here?" She needed a walk, needed a distraction, hadn't indulged in any art in a long time, and figured that if she got lucky, she could maybe find a piece to deface for revenge. She grinned. "Nah, not the artist's fault the Douchestone family funded the wing."

It was a brisk, ten-block walk and she loved every step. The sun was shining; the buildings were handsome; the sidewalks were lined with trees, and it was warm enough that she didn't feel like she should have worn fifteen layers.

She was delighted when she arrived at the museum, a redbrick building in the heart of downtown. Out in Blackstone, she really was starved for culture, and for the first time since moving there, actually starting to regret that decision. *Maybe I don't need peace and quiet all the time.* And now that she was semi-homeless after the brawl with Drew, maybe it was time to consider relocation—again.

She paid the museum entrance fee, collected her map, and eagerly entered the space. The first room had contemporary sculptures, with lots of found materials and carved wood. Another room had some fantastic ceremonial masks from various Pacific Northwest First Nations peoples like the Chinook and Tlingit. Admiring the deep reds and blacks on the face of a beaver mask, she thought, *Hm, maybe I should add a new category to my antiques repertoire.*

Crossing from one showroom to another, she passed by what looked more like a perpetual PR campaign than an actual exhibit. The far wall bore a quote:

> *"Art is the fabric of culture and it is our duty to bring it to the masses."*
> —Gloria Blackstone

Nice pat on the back there, Gloria. Under the quote there was a stand with a giant volume. "What kind of book is that?" She walked over to it and opened it to the middle.

Each page had a select set of mementos from that year's Blackstone Family Trust Annual Gala held in the ballrooms of various hotels. There were programs for the evenings, menus, a few pictures with the dignitaries of the day, and always one large picture of the current Blackstone family members involved in the event and what looked like the entire event staff, including from the hotel and the catering company. There were captions identifying the Blackstone family members and key staff members, such as the hotel's manager and the cooks who had handled the catering.

Intrigued with this little slice of the family's history in the community, she flipped back a few pages. She was now in the mid-nineteen sixties. In the group picture of sixty-five, she saw a young man, Francis, looking much younger than Jordan, whom she guessed was Jordan's grandfather or grand-uncle. *I wonder if they're in here*. She flipped back even more, past the fifties, forties, and thirties.

Reaching the mid-twenties, she saw group pictures featuring Marcus. He wore a particularly self-satisfied smirk. "Wonder what that's about."

She flipped back two more, to 1919. The gala was spectacular, with the men in tuxedos and the women in flowing white dresses. The Blackstones present in this picture, Gloria and Reginald, were just to the right of the center of the photo.

From his bright smile, Katherine felt like this must have been the ascendancy of Reginald's young life. He looked like he was in his very late teens or early twenties. She guessed he was most likely being prepared to take his place in the family business. Also, for this era, he was probably considered to be of prime marrying age.

"Huh. Gloria died the very next year. Must've been hell on the two boys."

Her gaze moved to the faces on Reginald's left. There was a balding, middle-aged man, likely the hotel's manager; a man looking to be in his thirties in a chef's hat, probably the caterer; and then...

She gasped. *It's her!*

A beautiful young woman with long, dark hair, bright eyes, and a brighter smile stood proudly next to the head chef. Katherine didn't know how she knew, but she had no doubt at all. *Is it her build? Her facial structure?* She couldn't put her finger on it, but this woman was the one whose spirit she'd encountered.

She found the corresponding name in the picture's caption. Eileen Byrne. Katherine pressed her index finger on Eileen's name. "Gotcha."

Katherine already had her phone out, but waited till she'd exited the museum before she called. "Kirk? I found her."

17

Katherine opened her arms to hug Kirk. "Thanks for meeting me."

He welcomed her embrace. "No problem, Kat."

They were meeting in that same Starbucks in which she'd initially contracted him and his crew. This time, though, she'd been more cognizant of his work schedule, so it was a little after sundown.

"What are you having?" She led him to the line.

"Oh, I'm just gonna have some tea," he said as he took out his wallet.

"No, no." She placed her hand on his wallet and gently pushed it away. "My treat for having put you through so much yesterday."

"You sure?"

"It's just tea, Kirk, can't be that expensive."

"You haven't seen what I ask them to do to my tea."

She ordered her usual hot cocoa and he got a chamomile. They then sat in chairs near to where they'd sat before.

As he blew the surface of his tea to cool it off, he offered, "So, your call sounded kind of..."

"Urgent?"

"No, I was gonna say excited."

"Yeah, I guess I am. After my encounter the night we all were at the mansion, I had no idea how I'd learn anything about her, and today, there she was!"

"This was the woman you saw right before I found you?"

"Yeah."

"And you recognized her from an old picture?"

"Uh-huh."

"Was it, like, one of those grainy, black-and-white, old-time-y photographs?"

"I mean, I dunno about all that. It was old, but professionally done. Why?"

"It's just kind of remarkable that after one encounter—"

"Pretty intense encounter."

"But that you'd be able to recognize her."

"I was amazed, too, but I know what I saw."

He shrugged. "Fair enough."

"You don't believe me."

"No, it's not that. I completely believe you believe you saw her, and I completely believe you believe you recognized her. But you have to admit, the whole thing is a little far-fetched."

THE HAUNTING OF BLACKSTONE MANSION

"Trust me, had you told me a week ago that this was gonna happen, I wouldn't have believed it either, but after what I saw?"

"So now that you know who she is, what are you gonna do next?"

"Right." She took out her phone and showed him a few web browser tabs she'd been checking out. "So, I found an unfortunately piss-poor amount on Ms. Byrne. No idea when she was born, where, though given how old she looked in the picture I saw at the museum, probably about 1900. Nothing about her early life. Looks like when she was about thirteen, she won some county fair baking contest." She stood, crossed to him, and knelt next to him. She tapped to a tab showing an old newspaper picture of Eileen, beaming with pride, standing behind her prize pie. "A few years after, she was working at the catering company that served the Blackstone gala."

"All sounds good so far."

"Yeah. Then there's this." She showed him another tab with another newspaper picture of Eileen and Reginald Blackstone, her in a nice dress, him in a suit. The headline read...

ENGAGEMENT OF MR. REGINALD BLACKSTONE AND
MS. EILEEN BYRNE

Katherine scrolled down to text that said...

```
wedding date set for June fifteenth.
```

"Nice," Kirk said. "So she moved up."

"She did, in fact, except…"

"Except?"

She lowered her phone. "No wedding."

"What do you mean?"

"There's no mention of it."

"You mean in the newspaper?"

"Anywhere!" She stood up, went back to her chair, and sat. "No pictures, no announcements, nothing of any kind."

"Maybe they just didn't broadcast it. Kept it a small affair."

"I thought about that, except why make such a big, splashy announcement about the engagement, and nothing about the actual wedding?"

He shrugged.

"That's not all," she continued. "Not only was a wedding never announced, but from when that engagement picture was taken, Eileen completely disappears from the historical record. No children, no society photos, no mention of her death. No grave site. She just vanishes."

"Maybe she was really private."

"Possibly, but look at this." She held up her phone. On it was an old obituary for Reginald Blackstone, the year 1921. "Reggie dies only two and a half years after his announced engagement to Eileen. Interestingly, exactly a year after his mother, Gloria."

THE HAUNTING OF BLACKSTONE MANSION

"So they're engaged, maybe no wedding, she disappears, and he dies."

"Doesn't that seem strange to you?"

"They could've broken up, and she disappeared into obscurity."

"Yeah. They could've, but something feels off. Like the Blackstones covered something up, or worse, ignored it."

"You think they murdered Eileen?"

"I think she died in that house."

"Why murder her, though?"

"I don't know, but if she did die there, even under mysterious circumstances, why wouldn't there have been a mention of her death? Some glamorous funeral of the Blackstone bride who almost was? Why just disappear?"

"You think if you solve her murder, she'll move on?"

"I think I need to go back to the mansion. Try and, I dunno, reach out."

"What makes you think she'll, uh, make contact?"

"Because now I'm not afraid; I just wanna help."

He nodded and got up. "I gotta hit the little boy's room."

"I'll be here." She set her phone on the chair's arm, put in her earbuds, and dialed Dean. It took a couple rings for him to pick up.

"Hey, Kat." His voice sounded different, more distant.

"Hey, guess what I'm gonna do?"

"What's that?"

"Ghost hunting."

"You're kidding me."

"Nope. I am tracking down Casper."

"Is this at that house?"

"Yep."

"So you *did* see a ghost?"

"Yep."

"Honey, are you feeling okay?"

"Fine, but I'll feel better once I've made contact. Again."

"Uh-huh, good luck with that."

She saw that Kirk was on his way back from the restroom. "Hey, Dean, I gotta go, otherwise I'll be rude to my friend."

"Friend? Or *friend?*"

"Friend, Dean. Bye." She picked up her phone. "You good to go?"

Kirk nodded. His face was clouded with concern. All traces of his usual good cheer had vanished. "Yeah."

"You okay? Now you're the one who looks like you've seen a ghost."

"Yeah, I'm good, Kat." He pointed to the door. "After you."

THE HAUNTING OF BLACKSTONE MANSION

Outside, she was ignoring his obvious mood change and trying to hype him up. "I think I'll head out sometime tomorrow morning. Not too early, but not near lunch."

He leaned up against his car and folded his arms. "What's your plan?"

"I dunno that I have one. I'll just go in and start talking to Eileen, see if she shows up, and if so, what she's willing to tell me, if anything."

He nodded, but said nothing.

"You should totally come!" she said. "If for no other reason but to prove me wrong, that all of this is in my head, that I didn't see anything."

He smiled politely. "Um, tomorrow's not great for me."

"Doesn't have to be tomorrow, could be Sunday."

"Whole weekend's kinda out for me."

He's blowing me off. Then again, ghost hunting isn't exactly a date. Get outta this now! "Yeah, I understand. Well, I'll let you know how it goes."

He was already getting into his car. "Sounds good, Kat." The way he said her name sounded so formal, as if they'd just met. "See you."

"See you, Kirk."

He pulled out and drove away so quickly, it was almost reckless. She stood there in the cold and growing dark of the Starbucks parking lot, then finally got in her car and drove back to Blackstone.

AUGUSTINE PIERCE

After picking up some burritos, salsa, chips, and tequila, Katherine returned to her motel room and laid out her feast on the table. She sat, opened a bag of blue tortilla chips, and ate one before she pushed the bag aside, got up, and grabbed her phone from next to the TV.

She stood in front of the TV and took deep breaths as she put her earbuds in. She tapped Kirk's number. He answered immediately.

"Hey, Kat." His voice was the same as before. Distant.

"Kirk, look, I'm sorry for inviting you out this weekend. I know that, after that night, after I was so inappropriate..."

"Kat?"

"No, let me finish. Look, Kirk, I like you. I know you didn't want to take advantage of me before, and I appreciate that. I really do. You're a good guy. And if you were interested, maybe we could do this the legit way, like have dinner or whatever. But obviously a ghost hunt is a little weird."

"It's not that."

"It isn't?"

"No."

"Is it the fact that I came on to you when I was outta-my-skull drunk?"

"No."

"Is it that you're just not into me?"

"On the contrary, I find you extremely attractive."

She felt suddenly and intensely excited. "So, what is it?"

"When you were talking to your friend?"

"Dean? Yeah?"

"I saw your phone."

She froze. *He knows.* "Kirk, I can explain if you just gimme a sec—"

"I looked you up, Kat."

"You what?"

"It wasn't hard. It came right up."

She closed her eyes with bitter regret. *Should've changed my goddamn name. Why didn't I change my name?*

"As much as I would love to have that dinner with you, I think right now what you need is space. And time."

No, I need you! "I see."

"You have a good night, Kat. And take care."

"You too, Kirk."

He hung up.

She stood there for what felt like hours, but was only a few seconds. She sat at her table of Mexican-inspired delights, but didn't have another bite. She instead called Dean.

"Dean?" Tears started to trickle down.

"Hey, listen, Kitten. It's not really a good time."

"D, I really need to talk to you."

"I know, honey. I know you do, but you can't."

"Why? Please tell me why."

Dean paused on the other end. "You know why, Kitten."

"I think I need to hear it. I think I'm ready."

They spoke at the same time.

"Because I'm..." he said.

"Because you're..."

"Dead." His voice faded into nothing, and all that was left was hers. "Little Kitten."

She didn't hang up because she had never called him at all. She'd merely been staring at his contact page, his smiling face, his name, his number, all his former details.

She opened a browser and googled their names, exactly as she imagined Kirk had done. The first result was a headline:

One Killed, One Injured in Freak Accident on Marquam Bridge.

At first, the tears only dripped. Then they rolled down her cheeks. Before she knew it, she was heaving heavy sobs. She ugly-cried for a solid three minutes. She hadn't cried this hard since that awful night, the night of the accident.

When she'd calmed a little, she set her phone down on the table next to the bag of chips. "What am I doing here? Why did I come here? What did I think I was gonna accomplish by running away? I can't help Eileen. I can't help myself. And now Kirk will never wanna talk to me again." She reached into the bag and took out a single chip. She dropped it in her mouth and chewed very slowly. "First thing tomorrow, I'll pack up, drive out to Portland, to a real hotel, stay in town long enough to give Jordan his check, then jump on the first flight back to New York."

She picked up the tequila bottle, twisted off the cap, and guzzled three hard slugs in one go. "But first, time to get friggin' trashed."

18

A sledgehammer repeatedly smashed into Katherine's head. Each time it cracked into her skull, it made the same shrill ringing sound. At least, that's how it felt. In reality, it was only her phone's alarm and the throb in her head from practically downing that bottle of tequila only a few hours earlier.

It was 11:00 in the morning and she had an hour to get packed up before the motel would kick her out. Under normal circumstances, that was more than enough time to get going, but how she was feeling now, she was lucky if she could drag her ass off the bed in under fifteen minutes.

Because her phone was still blaring, she not only dragged herself off the bed, but trudged the thousands of miles it felt like, to reach the TV so she could turn the little mind-crushing machine off.

She shut off her phone's alarm. She listened to the silence that now hung all around. *Oh my God, does that feel good.* She eyed the bed. It was so tempting.

THE HAUNTING OF BLACKSTONE MANSION

"No, you'll pass out, sleep through checkout, then the motel will threaten to have you arrested just like Drew and Jordan."

She opened her plastic grocery bag, set it on one end of the table, and shoved the pile of trash she'd produced last night into it. She knew it wasn't necessary. Motel staff would have cleaned it up, but even the sight of it made her feel worse about her current life outlook.

She stumbled over to the microscopic trash can near the TV. She tried to set the grocery bag of garbage into it, but the second she released her fingers, the can toppled over, dumping the contents everywhere.

She sighed hard. "Come on!" She leaned over to at least attempt to pick things up again, but immediately felt her head throb. "Screw it. It's the cleaning staff's job, so let them earn their keep."

She double-checked that she had everything, travel toiletries, phone, meager changes of clothes, jacket, and hobbled outside.

The sun stabbed her in the eyes. "You gotta be kidding me. Is it *always* that bright?" She opened her car and slumped into the driver's seat like a sack of potatoes. She closed the door so haphazardly that she had to do it again to make sure it had actually shut. She attempted to put on her seat belt, but the auto-lock mechanism kept thwarting her with its incessant *click, click, click!* She finally got it on, started up the car, and sat there. "Just one second."

She peered into the rearview. Her face looked like she'd been run over by a truck. "I can't go into the bank like this. Guess I'd better get myself a room before I do anything else."

She turned on the radio. Chipper bluegrass bounced out. "Eh, I can do country adjacent." With that, she got on the road.

Driving slower this time, it took her a full two hours to get into the city. Hitting Portland's downtown area, she scoured the blocks for a decent-looking hotel. After several turns down one-way streets, she finally spotted a classy-looking place, the Benson. She parked, walked in, and practically collapsed on the reception desk. "One room, queen's good, two, maybe three days."

The receptionist was very helpful, and within a minute, she was headed up to the third floor, where she quickly located her room, practically tore the door off its hinges, and collapsed on the bed.

Sleep did not come. "Oh come on!" She stared at the ceiling for another three minutes, then finally got up. "Guess I might as well get something to eat."

She went down to the first floor, located the hotel restaurant, and slouched in an open chair. When the server's soothingly calm voice asked for her order, she didn't feel like making things complicated, so she got a Caesar salad and orange juice.

As she munched her salad, her thoughts went around in circles on getting Jordan's check, giving it to him—*God, can I please skip that part?*—and Eileen. As much as Katherine just wanted to hightail it back to New York and go and find a rock to hide under, she couldn't stop thinking about Eileen.

Finished with her salad, she left the hotel, got in her car, and drove to the bank. She patiently waited in line for ten minutes. When it was her turn, she asked the teller about her check. It took a minute for the man to check, and with a frown, he informed her that it hadn't cleared yet and reiterated that it would take two or three business days.

"Of course. What was I thinking?" She left the branch, got into her car, and picked up her phone. She looked at things to do in the city. She made a list of muscums, art galleries, and bars.

She first drove back to the Portland Art Museum where she'd discovered Eileen's identity. She stayed there three hours, then returned to the Benson where she curled up to a documentary on the history of trains. She then got up, left the hotel, and walked to the South Park Blocks, a long strip of green space in the downtown area. She spent an hour walking all the way up their east side, then all the way down their west side. She then found a local independent movie theater that also served pizza and beer. She watched a film from six months ago. She hardly paid attention to the plot. She simply wanted to waste time.

Now a few minutes past ten, she walked to the Willamette River and watched the boats glide up and down. She walked back to the Benson, went up to her room, ordered room service, and watched another documentary, this time on the history of subway systems. She passed out around midnight.

Katherine slept in Sunday morning until ten. She checked her list of things to do and made a three-day itinerary, mostly of galleries, but also of Portland's historic places, and other points of interest such as its famous Japanese gardens.

Over the next three days, she switched between sleeping in to visiting some cultural site to returning to the Benson for lunch, watching a movie or visiting some other site in the afternoon, returning to the Benson for dinner, watching a documentary, and passing out.

It was now Wednesday morning when she called the bank again. After several prompts, the man on the other end of the phone informed her that the check had cleared.

THE HAUNTING OF BLACKSTONE MANSION

"Yes!" she declared with far too much excitement. She quickly got showered and dressed and ran downstairs. She jumped in her car and drove straight to the bank.

Arriving, she was half expecting that something else had gone wrong. To her amazement, the check was ready. All one hundred thousand smackeroos. For the first time in her life, she was delighted to be parting with so much money. *Now I don't owe you crap, Jordan.*

She got in her car and rang him. He picked up immediately.

"Kat!" He sounded shockingly happy, even deliriously so.

"Look, Jordan, I have no interest in wasting any more of your time. I've got your check. You there?"

"Yes, of course, yes, please, come on by. Can't wait."

She held her phone up to make sure she'd called the right person. "I'll, uh, see you in a few."

"Great! See you then." He hung up.

What the hell is going on? She drove straight to the Vista, parked, and rang his unit. He buzzed her in without even picking up. When she reached his door, she didn't hear his awful music blasting from inside. She knocked lightly three times. Footsteps ran to the door. There was a pause, likely him composing himself, and the door opened.

Jordan tried not to grin from ear to ear, but it was clear he was about to burst. "Kat, please come in! Can I get you something? I can order sushi again. Mackerel, right?"

"Jordan?"

"Please, please, sit down, make yourself comfortable."

"I'd really rather not. I have your check right here—"

"Please, I insist. Tea?"

She let out an exasperated exhale so loud she hoped he'd heard her. She sat. "Sure."

He brought over a tray of teacups, teas, and sugar. "I have something for you."

"What on earth could you possibly have for me?"

"You go first."

"Okay." She took out his check and offered it to him.

"Oh, you can set it down there." He pointed to the tea tray.

"All right." She lay the check on the tray.

"I'll get the water." He stood and went to the kitchen.

"Jordan, look, I'm exhausted and I've got about a million things I'd not only rather be doing, but need to be doing."

"Just one minute, Kat. I promise you'll like this." He returned with the kettle. He sat, poured each of them a full cup of hot water, and grabbed some green tea for himself. "Whatever you want."

"Thanks." She took another green tea.

"So, I owe you an apology."

"Accepted. Can I go now?"

He chuckled, but she was clearly trying his patience. "Just hold on, Kat."

"Fine."

"I know I've been challenging."

"One way to put it."

"You were right. I'm immensely insecure. You have to understand. I was born into a pile of money. Sent to the best schools. Pretty much guaranteed a job in the family business. But none of it was mine. I mean, yes, legally and monetarily speaking it was mine, but I hadn't *earned* any of it. I hadn't done anything of my own. So my whole life, I've been trying to find something that can be mine, that I can define for myself. I've never found it. I haven't done anything. So it's been a lifetime of living not only in my father's shadow, but literally everyone's shadow who came before him."

She nodded slowly, not sure what to say.

"So you were right, and I fully intend to figure out whatever I need to figure out for myself," he said.

"That's great, Jordan. I'm glad I could help." It was a mostly true statement, though she was still really itching to get out of there.

"So I apologize for being such a dick."

"Apology accepted." She meant it this time.

"The something I have for you." He stood, went back to the kitchen, and returned with two envelopes. They each had the word Katherine written in calligraphy. He handed her one. "You were absolutely right. You earned it."

She opened the envelope and took out a check for twenty thousand dollars.

"I stand by ten percent being the wrong number." He grinned.

"That's great, Jordan. Thank you."

He handed her the second envelope.

She opened it to find what was clearly a legal document with his and her names written throughout. "What's this?"

"I had my attorneys draw that up."

"The ones you were gonna sic on me?"

"The same." He grinned. "You assessed and auctioned that one room, as promised, and even with the police confiscating my stuff—I've talked to them about that, by the way, and they're releasing it tomorrow—you got me the hundred K, so without the police or me getting in the way, I imagine you can do a lot more."

She held up the legal document. "Is this what I think it is?"

THE HAUNTING OF BLACKSTONE MANSION

"It's a contract for you to represent my estate, yes. That gives you my full permission to enter the grounds, bring whomever and whatever you need, make arrangements on my behalf, whatever. Show it to whomever you need. Oh, and of course, any auction-related expenses, moving antiques, cleaning, the estate will cover. Just send invoices and whatever."

"Including the recovered firearms?"

"Yep."

"Great. Guess I'd better give Chase a call."

"Chase?"

"The guy who bought the batch I had."

"Guess so."

"Um, when can I get started?"

"Whenever you want."

"Wow, I was about to get on a plane."

"Please don't, Kat. I need you on this. So as soon as you sign it..."

She set the contract on the tea tray. "I think I'll have my own attorney take a look, if you don't mind."

"No, of course. I totally understand."

"Jordan?"

"Yeah?"

"What else is going on?"

"What do you mean?"

AUGUSTINE PIERCE

"Look, don't get me wrong. I appreciate all this. I'm grateful, can't wait to get started, but it's a little Ebeneezer Scrooge Christmas morning."

He smiled. "That's fair." He stood, walked to his huge window overlooking the city, and stayed there silently, for a few seconds. "You absolutely called it. I spend way more than the trust provides, I'm a mid-list spinner at best, and the influencer thing, well, I can't even crack the top ten thousand in the US." He faced her. "To top it off, my latest gig? It was gonna be in Romania for some crazy Halloween fest. They dropped me. So now there's nothing coming in for a while."

"How long?"

"A *while*." He walked slowly back to the sunken area. "The cold, hard fact is I need you. If twenty percent isn't enough, I can go higher."

"That's not necessary."

"I need you to not only sell the mansion's antiques, but to help me figure out a way to monetize the property some other way, to, well, I dunno... I'm thinking Halloween attraction, haunted house sorta thing."

You have no idea. "I'm not really an expert on that, but I can certainly weigh in."

He looked immensely relieved. "Great! So, no more of this crap about flying back to New York, right?"

She lay back on the couch. "Well, I'll need to find an apartment and all that."

"I can help with that."

"Then I guess we have a deal."

"Fantastic."

She folded the contract, put it in her purse, and stood. "I guess I'll be talking to you soon."

"Great. Talk to you soon."

She nodded, said nothing else, and left.

19

What the hell am I gonna do now? Katherine was already driving back to Blackstone having canceled the rest of her stay at the Benson. *I was ready. I was gonna jump on a plane and get the hell outta here!* But twenty percent of, well, a lot, was still a lot.

She didn't even think she was going to have a lawyer look over Jordan's contract. She figured she'd google the language, and unless anything obviously untoward popped up, she'd just sign it and mail it back.

But because she had that contract, because she had a giant financial incentive to stay, she figured she might as well. For now.

After an hour, she found she was driving through Creek. The rental company was only a few blocks away from where she currently was, maybe another five minutes. *I shouldn't. No, I should! No, he'll think I'm stalking him. So what?* Without even fully making up her mind, she found she was driving straight to his office.

THE HAUNTING OF BLACKSTONE MANSION

She pulled into the parking lot and suddenly felt like she was meeting a guy for a date whom she fully expected to stand her up. Her adrenaline surged. She took several deep breaths, but that didn't make it better. She took a final, deep breath and got out of the car.

She walked up to the front door as if she were walking up the steps to the guillotine. *Maybe give some excuse: "I'm looking to rent another car." No, you arrived in a car that you bought from them. Um, "Can you guys recommend a local trail?" No! Why would you get trail recommendations from a car-rental company?* She entered, and before the bespectacled woman behind the desk—what was her name, Annie—had a chance to say anything, Katherine blurted, "Is Kirk here?"

Annie smiled at her as if she'd just heard a ton of juicy gossip about her. She leaned back in her chair and didn't turn around. "Oh, Kirk!" she said in a singsong voice.

Katherine's innards collapsed in dread. *Great. He's obviously told Annie I'm a goddamn psycho. And now I'm here, acting like a goddamn psycho.* She breathed slowly and tried to do it quietly, but Annie eyed her, so she must have heard her.

Kirk stepped out of the back office and regarded Katherine with what looked like curiosity, which was far better than fear or caution. "Hey, Kat, what can

I help you with?" His tone was formal, businesslike. He was keeping his distance.

I guess that's fair, all things considered. "Can I have just two minutes?"

"I don't know if that's such a good idea."

"Please, Kirk, just two minutes."

"Dude said no, bitch," Annie said.

Katherine ignored her.

"Annie, it's okay," Kirk said.

Annie lifted her eyebrows with incredulity, then typed something or other.

Katherine glanced out the front door. "Two minutes, then if you want, you'll never see me again."

Kirk nodded. "After you."

Katherine opened the door and held it for him. She then walked into the middle of the parking lot before turning around to face him. He'd followed her, but had kept a very polite distance of about four feet.

"So?" His tone was kind, if still formal.

"I'm not crazy. At least I don't think I am."

"Never thought you were crazy."

"Please, just let me finish while I still have the nerve."

He nodded.

"When Dean died, all our friends stopped talking to me," she recounted. "His husband, Ryan, threatened to sue me for wrongful death or criminal negligence or something... I don't even remember. My boyfriend got so sick of my constant crying and whining that he dumped me."

"I'm sorry."

She chuckled bitterly. "That last one was fine. We'd only been together a little while, wasn't going anywhere, and frankly, I was relieved when it was over." She paused to focus. "You have to understand that I'd met Dean in kindergarten and nothing could separate us, not high school, not different colleges. I was the first one he came out to. Before that, he was my first kiss. I was his best lady at his wedding. I loved him so much." Tears dripped down her cheeks. "And just like that"—she snapped her fingers—"he was gone. And along with him, pretty much my whole life. About two weeks after the funeral—which I attended, but I stood apart from everyone else, kept my distance—I called his old number. Not for any reason, just to... I guess, go through the motions, to have something, *anything* that reminded me of him. I talked to him, and in my mind, he talked back. Next day, I did it again, and again, and again. Before I knew it, I was hooked. It *felt* like I was talking to him, so I just kept doing it. I pretended to dial, pretended to hear the ring, the buzz, the voicemail prompt. Hell, I even pretended to hear the three-beep hanging up. Anything that let me believe, for just one second, that he was still with me."

"I understand."

"I know he's not really there. I know I'm not really talking to him, but it's been the closest thing, so what you saw the other day"—she shrugged—"that's what that was."

He nodded. "What about the Eileen sighting?"

She smiled. "Surprised you remember her name."

"'Course I do."

"I don't know what to say, Kirk. I was positive I saw... what I thought I saw. Maybe I was wrong. Maybe I was tired. I don't know. If that's enough for you to never wanna see me again, I understand, but know that I *wasn't* making it up. I *thought* I saw something."

"Katherine, I admit I was freaked out. I appreciate your explanations. I still think you need time, but it doesn't have to be 'never again.'"

Tears started down her cheeks all over again. "Okay."

He walked up to her and wiped her cheeks with his sleeve. "I'm really sorry about Dean."

"Thank you."

"Unfortunately, I should probably..." He pointed inside.

"Yeah, I understand."

He stepped back.

THE HAUNTING OF BLACKSTONE MANSION

"I'm heading out to Blackstone mansion Saturday, probably morning," she said. "If you happened to, coincidentally, drop by and maybe join me for lunch, that wouldn't be so bad."

He walked backward to the office. "No, it wouldn't."

"Then maybe I'll see you."

He smiled. "You might just. Later, Kat."

"Later, Kirk."

He went inside. She wiped her cheeks again and her eyes. She got into her car, drove back to Blackstone, back to the motel, and checked in for another few nights.

Katherine spent the next two days looking up potential apartments, considering it looked like she was planning to stay in the Blackstone area, at least for now. She had to find something close enough to the mansion, so it wouldn't be a pain to drive out to it, but far enough from the town she wouldn't have the chance of bumping into Drew, or Bobby from Sean's Bar and Grill.

She also faced the problem that her recent rental history wasn't exactly stellar, and by now probably well-known in the town, so she could either explain herself to any potential landlords or just pretend she hadn't been evicted from her last place. *I never signed anything so there's no record.*

She found three possibilities, all within an hour's drive of the mansion, the managers sounded skeptical once the question of her current employment situation came up.

In the end, she realized that she may have to take Jordan up on his offer for help, even though she wasn't entirely sure what that meant. Would he simply put in a good word with some landlord he happened to know or did he have a property he hadn't mentioned that he'd either let her rent for a reduced rate or for free? *There's the mansion. No way. Not living there. No electricity, probably no running water. And knowing him, he'd make me fix all of it.*

By Friday evening, after having googled Jordan's contract, signing it, and sending it back to him, she settled in for another night of tequila and snacks, though she had no intention on getting as plastered as she had before.

Saturday morning, Katherine got up at ten, showered, and headed out to the local grocery store, where she picked up some sandwiches and drinks for a simple lunch up at the mansion. While she didn't expect to spend all day up there, she was sure she'd be there at least a few hours. Now that she had Jordan's official permission to be there, she fully intended to take in every last detail.

Heading up the hill, she regarded the ever-present twilight that hung in the woods around the mansion as a sort of challenge, as if it were daring her to come back, daring her to face its dark secrets. "I'm comin' for ya," she warned the woods.

She pulled up to the gate and parked. It was strange seeing that bold, black brick wall. The last time she'd been here, she was desperate to leave with no intention of ever coming back. Now, she almost couldn't wait to get back inside.

She got out of the car and practically strutted up to the gate. "I see you, Blackstone mansion." She slipped through the gate and confidently hiked up the road.

When she reached the top of the hill, she didn't hesitate as she headed up the front steps with a *tap, tap, tap* of her feet on the stone. She threw open the right door and stepped in as if she were the house's new owner.

A silver glint. She saw it on the floor. She took out her flashlight and turned it on. The mansion's entryway was as dark and quiet as ever. Artemis and Apollo still looked like they might glare and cackle at her at any second. But for the first time since she'd first stepped foot in here, she felt no fear.

AUGUSTINE PIERCE

She took slow, determined steps, scanning the floor for whatever might pop into her peripheral vision. She took out Jordan's contract and held it up as if to show the house. "If anyone's here, Gloria, Eileen, I have every right to be here. Your great-whatever-grandson gave me his permission. Officially. If you are here, Eileen, I'd like to talk. I don't know if I can help, but I wanna try." She stopped and let out a little gasp.

Her light had landed on the cake stand that she'd found in the attic and had held that first day she'd wandered in here. She stared at it a moment as if it were about to leap off the floor and attack her. She closed in on it until she was standing directly over it. "I'm gonna pick this up." She bent over, and as she did, she happened to notice that she was standing halfway between the front doors and the staircase. She looked around and noticed that she was also halfway between the east side of the entryway and the west. *I'm directly in the middle. That's intention.* "So I'm gonna pick this up, all right?"

She lifted the cake stand off the floor and held it with a certain reverence, as if she were presenting her own cake to a royal client. She checked the base. Those initials: E+R. "Eileen plus Reginald." She waited. She heard nothing, saw nothing, and felt nothing. She spoke to herself, "You must've put it here for *some* reason."

THE HAUNTING OF BLACKSTONE MANSION

She stopped talking when she felt the metal above her fingertips, the side of the stand facing away from her, grow colder. To make sure it wasn't her imagination, she reached out with her right hand to touch both sides of the stand to compare. The far side was much colder. "You want me to go up the stairs?"

No one responded.

She took two steps toward the stairway. The chill faded from the cake stand. She stopped. She took one step back. She now felt the stand's side closest to her cool a little. It wasn't the same intense cold as the opposite side had been before, but it was noticeable. "Wait, are we playing hot and cold only now it's cold and cold?"

No one answered her.

"Not the stairs, obviously not out the front doors." She turned to her right and took a step forward. The far side of the stand got much colder. She nodded and grinned. "I gotcha. After you, Eileen." Katherine walked forward a few steps. Each time she took a new step, she paused to see if the same part of the stand remained cold, pointing her in that direction. With her fifth step forward, she distinctly felt the chill of the stand's side facing away from her shift to her left.

She stopped and looked left. It was the door to the right of the staircase. *There something special in there?* She suspected there wasn't since she'd already explored the following rooms and other than their varying functions—drawing room, music room, smoking room—there was nothing particularly odd about them.

She turned left and walked forward. As she did so, the cold in the stand's metal moved back to the side facing away from her, a sign that she was going in the right direction. With a little more confidence in her and Eileen's rudimentary communication, she walked forward a little faster till she reached the door. "It's in here, right?"

She heard no response.

"I'll take that as a maybe." She opened the door into that first hallway that led to the main west-east hall. "This is that first hallway that led me to the kitchen."

The stand's chill moved from the side away from her to her right. She turned and headed down the hallway. "Are you taking me to the kitchen?"

No one answered.

She had nearly reached the kitchen when she felt the cold abruptly disappear from the side of the stand facing away from her. She then felt the stand's left side cool quickly and intensely. She stopped and yanked away her left hand. "Ow! Careful!"

She heard no apology.

She turned left, facing the west tower. She walked slowly down the hallway. She passed the kitchen door. She approached the next door. The instant she stood right in front of it, she felt the entire cake stand base cool. She faced the door. "I understand."

She opened the door to find a grand dining room with a great long table seated with five chairs down its length and one chair at each head. "What's in here?"

She heard the same sound as she had days ago up in the attic of the west tower. It was a low, wheezing whine. She at first heard it throughout the room, as if it were coming from some modern, unseen speaker system. Then she heard it move and localize in front of her and to her right, near the far end of the table.

She took slow steps toward the sound. As she did, it calmed from a whine to more of a guttural groan.

Then it ceased, and there was silence for a few seconds. "Eileen?"

Pop! Crack! It sounded like a chef snapping the backbone of a chicken carcass. She shone her flashlight in the area where she thought she was hearing these new sounds.

A small, oily black cloud floated in the air about a half a foot above where the table stood. Fleshy tendrils of bone and sinew sprung forth from it. The tendrils grew, thickened, and sprouted more of themselves until a head-sized mass of what looked like bone and desiccated flesh hung in midair. Had she not been so fascinated with what she was witnessing, she would have been completely disgusted.

The flesh and bone mass had now grown into what resembled a human torso with stumps where the neck, arms, and legs would have been. In the lower portion of the torso, the pulsing black mass remained. Soon those stumps grew into their respective missing appendages. She focused her beam on the rising neck. Muscle tissue and tendons crawled up over chunks of skull. Before she knew it, a partially decomposed, thoroughly desiccated mummy of a person stood before her. The fracture remained across the forehead and eye sockets.

"Eileen? Is that you?"

Crack! The skull twisted to face her.

Katherine let out a tiny, startled gasp.

The monstrous, undead face she'd seen the other evening in the attic now had half-formed, milky eyes that gleamed a sickening white in the beam of the flashlight. The jaw *creaked* open. A dusty, *hissing croak* eked out.

Katherine breathed slowly, still not entirely sure what to make of all this. She set the cake stand down on the table and pointed to herself. "I'm Katherine. I came here to sell your great-great-grand-nephew's belongings, the stuff in this mansion, but if there's some way I can help you, please, show me."

Eileen's corpse took two *snapping, crackling* steps toward her. Katherine looked down at those skeletal feet, as if their function were new to her.

"You don't have to walk all the way," Katherine said. "Let me help you."

The corpse stopped moving. It raised its left palm in a gesture that looked like it was warning her to stay away.

Katherine nodded. "All right, I'll stay here."

The corpse twisted and stumbled as if struggling against some crushing, unseen force. With a brief *hiss*, it faded into the darkness in a puff of black smoke.

Katherine scanned the space before her with her flashlight. "Eileen? Where did you go? Hello?" She heard another *crackling hiss* from behind her. She spun around to find the corpse standing next to the door she'd entered. It lifted its right arm and held it against the door.

Katherine nodded. "I think I understand." She walked back to the door, and as she approached it, the corpse again vanished. She exited into the hallway, but didn't see the corpse anywhere. "Eileen? Am I going back to the entryway? Down this hall?"

In the distance to her right, toward the west tower, she heard the corpse's *hiss*. She walked quickly down the hallway, where she saw it in front of the west tower's doors right before it vanished. She opened the right door, but didn't see the corpse inside. "In here?"

There was no hiss or any other sound.

She recognized the spiral staircase she'd raced up to investigate the light in this tower's attic. She shone her flashlight's beam all around. She spotted the triangular pattern with its missing left corner and V-shaped lower portion. She made a mental note to check that out later. She then focused her light on the staircase. "Am I going back up there? Did they stuff you in the ceiling?"

A *groaning hiss* rose from the other side of the room. There, her beam found the corpse standing with its back up against the wall. Its skull twitched. Its limbs jerked.

Katherine slowly walked toward it. "Am I going there?"

The corpse made no noise, movement, or gesture.

Katherine continued her approach, though she now felt a rising sense of danger. *What's she doing?* "Are you gonna show me something?"

The vertebrae of the neck *cracked* as the skull lowered and raised in a sort of nod.

Katherine had almost reached the corpse. Although she had offered to help it walk, her survival instincts were taking over, and the thought of touching this thing was making her stomach churn. "What are you gonna show me? What happened?"

THE HAUNTING OF BLACKSTONE MANSION

The skull didn't move.

Katherine was now about two feet away from it. "Help me, Eileen. What happened here?"

The corpse seized her arm with incredible strength and yanked her up against it. The right side of Katherine's face pressed into its rib cage. The flesh was freezing.

Katherine shouted. "Aahh!"

The corpse wrapped its bony fingers around the back of her head and thrust her face to the floor.

Everything went black.

20

What's going on? Where am I? Katherine saw nothing but black and felt nothing but numb cold. Unlike feeling the icy breeze when she first arrived in Blackstone, this cold didn't bother her, didn't feel like it would freeze her the longer she soaked in it.

She moved her arms and legs around as if she were dog paddling in a lake, but she felt no wet and didn't see any of her limbs, not even her arms when she moved them where she thought they would be right in front of her face.

She tried to call out, *Hello? Hello!* but she only heard her voice in her head. She felt nothing escape her lips.

A pinpoint of light. It looked like it was incredibly far away, miles and miles, but when she instinctively paddled toward it, if that's what it could be called in this strange space, the pinpoint grew larger and brighter. Then, as if slipping down a waterslide, the pinpoint grew to the size of a golf ball, a basketball,

THE HAUNTING OF BLACKSTONE MANSION

and finally two bright horizontal cones of light that started from two small points next to each other on her right and spread out to her left till they stopped at what looked like a flat surface, a floor, and most of a wall.

She saw shapes, figures, people. She couldn't make out any details yet, but she saw heads and bodies and legs. As the vision drew nearer, she could hear muffled, distant voices. It was polite conversation sprinkled with laughter.

The scene was clearer now. It was the Blackstone family's dining room. It was a grand, warm, inviting space with its gold-and-crimson tablecloth and the finest soups, salads, and meats. She even spotted the cake stand right in front of Reginald. *Oh my God, there it is!* Two butlers stood in attendance against the wall to the left. Gloria sat at the end of the table facing Katherine's view. To Gloria's right sat Reginald, then Marcus. Opposite Gloria, Katherine saw a silhouette that looked to be in the shape of Vernon. And opposite Reginald sat...

That was when Katherine realized it. Everything she was seeing must have been through Eileen's eyes. The only parts of Eileen she could see were her hands occasionally lifting in front of where her eyes would be—the sources of the cones of light. Everything outside Eileen's field of vision was completely black. No shadows, no dust, only black.

AUGUSTINE PIERCE

"It's going to be wonderful, Mother," said an overeager Reginald. "I'm taking Eily on a steamer to London, Paris, Rome, possibly even to Istanbul. It will be a trip for the ages, and when we return, she'll be so in demand in all the courts of Europe that she'll be the most famous pastry chef in the world."

"I don't know about all that, Reggie," Eileen's nervous voice said. "I would love to see Rome, though. The Vatican? I've seen pictures and it looks so glorious."

"Pastries?" Gloria looked straight down her nose at something she was about to pick up.

She lifted her hand from behind the cake stand. Her fingers clutched on to a supremely fashioned cake knife. From its point to the end of its handle, it had been fashioned as a single smoothly flowing piece. Its surface was decorated with a matching pattern, of sunflowers and roses, to that of the cake stand, with the monograph E+R stamped on its blade.

"Cakes, pies, and pastries, then?" As she turned the knife over and over between her fingers, Gloria wouldn't even look in Eileen's direction.

What's going on here? Is she gonna stab that thing into her eye? Is that how she died? Katherine floated her way past Vernon and his sons, to Gloria's side. The entire right side of Gloria's body, out of Eileen's sight line,

THE HAUNTING OF BLACKSTONE MANSION

was all black, but everything else, Katherine could see perfectly.

"Yes, Mrs. Blackstone," Eileen said. "All that and more. I also hope to further my education in the French and Italian traditions. Éclairs, *latti inglesi*. All of it."

"Am I to understand, then, Ms. Byrne, that with my dear Reginald's hand, you intend to"—Gloria cocked an eyebrow—"serve pastries to the courts of Europe for, what, a year... two?"

"Mother," Reginald said in a warning tone, likely recognizing her condescension.

Gloria placed her right hand over Reginald's fingers that were curling into fists. She easily kept flipping the cake knife over and over in only her left hand. "Oh, don't fuss, Reginald. It's so unbecoming. I was merely asking the girl a question as to her ambitions."

"In fact, Mrs. Blackstone, I don't intend to serve the courts exclusively," Eileen elaborated.

"Oh?" Gloria cocked her eyebrow again.

"No, Mrs. Blackstone," Eileen said. "I intend to serve the poor and rich alike."

Reginald fidgeted with excitement. "Eily is quite the egalitarian, Mother."

"Is that so?" Gloria gave her son a condescending smile.

"I think it's a capital idea!" Vernon interjected.

AUGUSTINE PIERCE

Finally, a little support for Eileen. Katherine moved in between Marcus and Vernon to get a closer look at Vernon. Despite the stuffiness that his portraits had shown, he seemed to be a pretty easygoing guy.

"Do you, now, dear?" Gloria asked.

"Why not bring the cakes to the people?" Vernon asked. "It's bound to happen eventually. Look at the automobile! Why, George predicts that within twenty years, everyone will own one!"

Both Gloria and Marcus chuckled.

"Oh, please, Vernon." Gloria shook her head.

"Honestly, Father, automobiles? Everyone?" Marcus asked.

"After the wedding, we intend to open a shop downtown," Reginald bragged. "Eily will be the head chef. She'll design all the pastries, Mother."

"Will she, then?" Gloria almost looked at Eileen. "And how was she planning on funding this little culinary endeavor?"

"My trust is to come due when I turn twenty," Reginald said.

Now Gloria was losing her grip on her already thin polite veneer. "You intend to spend your trust on a... a bakery?"

"In fact, Mrs. Blackstone, I've saved a bit of my own," Eileen said. "I plan to invest as well."

THE HAUNTING OF BLACKSTONE MANSION

"Well, all this talk of sweets has given me quite a hankering for dessert!" Gloria slammed the cake knife down on the table.

At that instant, both butlers in Eileen's sight line, along with two outside it, rushed out of the room in as professional a manner as possible.

What the hell is going on?

Marcus sounded particularly annoyed. "Where are they off to?"

Gloria stood. "I won't be a moment." She strutted into the darkness behind Eileen.

She going to the kitchen? Why? Isn't she the lady of the house?

Eileen spoke quietly to Reginald, "I don't think she likes me."

Reginald took her hand and squeezed it lovingly. "Darling, she doesn't even like me."

He and Eileen giggled.

"A bakery!" Vernon exclaimed. "Downtown! What do you think, Marcus?"

"I have no opinion on the matter, Father."

A dozen kitchen staff marched past Eileen, out the room.

"Where on earth are they off to?" Marcus asked.

Katherine heard stomping footsteps behind Eileen.

"If I had wanted to purchase myself a trollop, I would have ventured into the red light!" As Gloria finished her exclamation, a thin rope came down over Eileen's face, was wrapped around her neck, and pulled tight.

Eileen could only see flashes of the others as her field of vision bounced and stuttered with her struggle against Gloria's grip.

Katherine ran to Eileen's side. *Fight her, Eileen! Kick her off!*

Reginald and Vernon launched to their feet, and raced to Eileen.

"Mother! Have you gone mad?" Reginald demanded.

"Gloria! What's the meaning of this?" Vernon asked.

Eileen saw hardly anything clearly, but it looked like both Reginald and Vernon were struggling to tear Gloria off her.

Marcus stayed put and leaned back in his chair, looking quite amused.

Gloria yanked as hard as she could against Eileen's neck. "I will *not* watch my firstborn obliterate his birthright on such wanton frivolity!"

Eileen's feet kicked.

She's losing. She's gonna pass out! Do something, Reginald!

Suddenly, Katherine heard the sound of flesh on flesh with a *smack* as Vernon knocked Gloria off Eileen. "That's enough, Gloria!"

THE HAUNTING OF BLACKSTONE MANSION

Eileen collapsed. While Katherine heard Vernon and Gloria grunt as he fought to hold her back, Eileen crawled her way to the table and slowly climbed up to her feet. *Crash!* She pulled the tablecloth and many of the platters down with it. All she could see were portions of the floor, parts of the table, and a pair of arms helping her to her feet.

"Get off me!" Gloria roared.

Katherine futilely searched the darkness behind Eileen to see what Gloria was up to, what she was referring to, but it was impossible. Anything that Eileen couldn't see, Katherine couldn't see either. She heard Vernon groan, then a body collapse on the floor. *Did Gloria... kill him?*

Eileen bent over the table, catching her breath and coughing.

"Come, my darling," Reginald insisted. "Quickly. Let's go. Mother's gone mad."

Eileen lifted her head when she heard the same footsteps stomp up behind her as before.

"Get up!" Gloria shoved Reginald aside. He tripped backward, and fell flat.

"Mother! No!" Reginald cried.

Eileen swiped a fork from the table. She spun around, pointed the fork in the direction where she thought Gloria was standing, and swung.

Feet away, she saw Vernon on the floor, his hands buried between his legs. Reginald slowly got back on his feet. Marcus stood safely away from the commotion.

Eileen's attack was completely off. Not one scratch landed on Gloria's face or arms.

"Pathetic!" Gloria backhanded Eileen with such viciousness, Katherine assumed the woman had done so to dozens of servants, and perhaps even her own children, countless times before.

Eileen fell back against the table.

Come on, Eileen. Please! Get up! Reginald, do something!

Reginald stumbled to Eileen and Gloria. "Mother!"

With her own determined grunt, Eileen shoved herself off the table. She swung for Gloria, but the older woman was ready. She caught Eileen's fist and punched her square in the jaw with the other hand.

Eileen hit the table again. She groaned at the pain throbbing all the way from her temples down to her neck. She slowly turned her head to face the family. Vernon struggled to stand. Reginald reached Eileen's side, and wrapped his arm around hers.

Marcus rushed to Gloria's side. "Are you all right, Mother?"

Gloria flexed her punching hand. "Nothing a little ointment won't cure." She picked up a knife from the table, wrenched Reginald off Eileen, grabbed

THE HAUNTING OF BLACKSTONE MANSION

her by the hair, and twisted her around to face the men.

Eileen struggled against Gloria, but Katherine could tell her strength was waning.

Just run. Just get the hell outta here!

With her fist still fiercely gripping Eileen's hair, Gloria yanked her head back, exposing her neck, and placed the knife on her stomach.

Reginald stepped back, likely having no clue how to safely free Eileen from Gloria's grip.

Vernon limped toward the women. "This is insanity, Gloria! Let the poor girl go!"

Eileen couldn't see whether Gloria was glaring at her husband, but her bitter tone said all that was necessary. "Admit it, Vernon. Admit it or I gut her like a goddamn sow!" Gloria demanded.

"Admit what?"

"Father, what's Mother talking about?" Reginald's eyes searched for a way to easily help Eileen escape.

"Admit it!" Gloria ordered. "Admit that you betrayed me and your family, thirty years of marriage, for this cheap Irish bitch!"

"Gloria, please!" Vernon exclaimed. "You're the only woman I've ever loved!"

"Admit it or I cut out her entrails right now!"

"Vern, please!" Eileen begged.

AUGUSTINE PIERCE

To prove she was serious, Gloria cut into Eileen's dress deep enough that Eileen saw the patch around the knife stain red.

"Don't hurt her, Gloria! I beg you," Vernon said.

"Do you admit it?"

"We didn't mean for it to happen."

"Father, what are you talking about?" Reginald stepped even farther back from Eileen.

Vernon ignored his son. "I only wanted to acquaint myself with the woman my son intended to marry. I never expected..."

"Eileen?" Reginald's voice hung with desperation.

"I'm so sorry, Reggie. I never meant to fall in love with your father," Eileen wept.

"That's disgusting!" Marcus cackled.

"You cheap whore!" Reginald hit Eileen as hard as he could.

She hit the floor and did not move.

Katherine heard Gloria put the knife back on the table.

"Did he kill her?" Marcus sounded intensely intrigued.

"Don't be stupid," Gloria scoffed. "Your brother didn't strike her hard enough for that."

"Oh, my sweet darling," Vernon said.

Eileen saw his knees appear to her right.

At least he cares a little.

"How could you, Father?" Reginald whined. "You knew that I loved her."

Vernon helped Eileen to her feet. "That's it, darling. All will be well. I'll take you back to the city. Everything will be well."

"Are you really such a dumb Dora?" Gloria asked. "You can't possibly be seen with her!"

"I won't leave her here!"

"Vernon, if anyone sees you and her together, alone, the scandal will end us!"

"Please, Vern, let's just run away," Eileen said. "You and I. I love you so much."

"No!" Reginald swiped the cake knife from off the floor, shoved his father aside, and plunged it as deep as it could go into Eileen's gut.

Eileen gasped, but otherwise made little sound.

No! All Eileen saw was her arms held up to shield herself. All Katherine could hear was sharp metal slicing into flesh.

"No!" Vernon tore his son off Eileen. She collapsed to her knees, then keeled over onto her side. He scooped her up in his arms.

Katherine could clearly hear Eileen whisper, "It's yours."

"Please, don't try to talk, my darling," Vernon said as he cried.

"What did she say?" Marcus asked.

"It doesn't matter," Gloria said. "Get rid of her."

AUGUSTINE PIERCE

"But, Mother, where?" Reginald asked.

Smack! Katherine heard what sounded like the back of Gloria's hand against Reginald's cheek. "Anywhere!" Gloria snarled.

"But we... I... If we..." Reginald stammered.

"The cemetery," Marcus said coolly.

Vernon let Eileen down long enough to bark at his family. "What? No!"

"In one of the older graves. Great-grandfather's. No one would ever think to look there."

"I won't let you. She deserves a proper burial."

She's not even dead, you prick! Help her!

Gloria stepped up to her husband. "Marcus, you'll take her." She turned to face him. "Silas's grave."

"No, Mother, I'll go," Reginald said.

"Both of you. Go now," Gloria eased Vernon away from Eileen.

The next thing Eileen saw was the brothers standing over her. Reginald already looked deeply remorseful and heartbroken. *A tragic fit of teenage rage.* Marcus, though, looked calm, pleased. If Katherine didn't know better, she would have guessed that he was having the time of his life with all this murder and conspiracy.

"Here," Gloria said, but Eileen didn't see what she was referring to.

The brothers bent over her. Her view rolled to the right ninety degrees, then back to the left. *A stretch-*

THE HAUNTING OF BLACKSTONE MANSION

er? Marcus stepped away. Katherine heard a tiny snapping sound. A small, flickering light appeared to Eileen's left. *A match? What are they lighting?* A solid, much brighter light swelled over the entire room. Marcus stepped back into view, now carrying a lit lantern. *How far out are we going?* From the shaking in Eileen's sight lines, Katherine guessed they were lifting her up.

Yards and yards of ceiling then passed by. Finally, they marched out open double doors into the rain.

Eileen saw the pale light of a nearly full moon peeking through black treetops every few seconds and an endless stream of sadly drooping branches trickling shimmering drops onto her face.

Reginald cried again, "We can't do this."

"Quiet, Reg," Marcus ordered calmly.

Eileen's vision was fading. Momentary spasms of black clouded it.

No. God, not in the middle of the woods.

Time passed, but Katherine couldn't tell how long.

The brothers stopped moving. Blackness clouded Eileen's vision more frequently.

Only seconds now.

The brothers set Eileen down. She didn't see where they were going, but Katherine heard both their footsteps walk away.

"Here," Marcus said.

"Why do I have to do it?" Reginald asked.

"You're stronger, so it'll go faster."

"Could've brought two."

"Well, we didn't. Now dig."

Katherine heard a shovel stab into the moist earth and toss its contents aside. This went on for what felt like a good long time, though miraculously, Eileen's vision didn't completely fade.

The brothers' faces appeared again. With a jerk, they lifted Eileen and tossed her into her shallow grave. Reginald stepped out of her sight lines. The shovel stabbed into the ground again. Piles of dirt flew in from the right. Eileen's vision was soon almost completely obscured. All movement ceased.

"Let's go," Reginald's voice wallowed in despair.

"Wait." Marcus held up his hand.

"What?"

"Look."

"What?"

"Her eyes."

"What about them?"

"Look closely." Marcus stepped into the grave next to Eileen and got down uncomfortably close to her face. He shone the lantern right next to her right eye.

Katherine could see his creepy, angular face more clearly than she'd been able to so far. His lips twisted up in a cruel smirk. *Wish I could smack that smug right off his lips. Kick him, Eileen!*

"She's blinking." Marcus stood up.

THE HAUNTING OF BLACKSTONE MANSION

"No, she's not," Reginald denied, though Katherine could hear in his voice that he also saw it.

"Yes, she is, look!"

"She's not."

"Would you just look, Reg?"

Reginald sighed with deep annoyance, but walked over to Eileen's other side and crouched. "She'll be dead soon enough."

"Mother wants this done now."

Reginald glared at his brother. "I already stabbed her."

"Fine. I'll do it myself." Marcus stepped out of the grave. When he returned to Eileen's field of vision, he was holding the shovel. "Outta the way."

Reginald obeyed and stepped back.

No. Please, no.

Marcus raised the shovel high above his head. Even in Eileen's fading, darkening vision, Katherine could easily see how deeply Marcus was relishing this. His eyes gleamed. His smirk grew into a nasty smile.

The shovel plunged straight into Eileen's field of vision. Over and over and over again. The first time Marcus yanked it out, Katherine spied a glistening crimson streak along its muddy edge. The second, the streak had thickened into dripping globs. The third, gray speckles clung to the gore. Blackness soon overtook everything.

AUGUSTINE PIERCE

Eileen was gone.

21

Katherine sat up with a gasp. She was still on the floor in the west tower where Eileen's corpse-ghost had brought her. "Oh my God! Oh my God!" Before she knew what was happening, she keeled over onto her hands and knees and vomited.

She took a deep breath. "Oh my God." She wiped her mouth on her jacket sleeve. "The cemetery. Eileen's still out there." She picked up her purse, dug out her flashlight, and clicked it on. She struggled to stand, stumbled several feet, and almost fell twice.

She finally found her footing and ran down the hallway, straight out the entryway. Outside, she felt disoriented for a second. Flashes of what Eileen's ghost had shown her still rattled around in her head.

She turned off her flashlight and put it back in her purse. She stood still and tilted her head back. Recognizing the view from the vision, she retraced a few steps. Her right hand jolted toward the left door so she wouldn't fall on her posterior. "We went right."

AUGUSTINE PIERCE

She started off to her right, the mansion's west side. At first she had no clue where to go. All the trees looked the same. She tipped her head back again. That didn't help. All the treetops looked the same too.

She stopped. "We went this way." She oriented herself to roughly where her back faced the west side of the mansion. She decided this was the right direction. She hadn't seen further details of the mansion after they'd exited it, so they must have moved away from it. Deeper into the woods.

She eagerly ran down the hill, though not so fast that she'd trip. After only a few seconds, she saw a metallic-looking, man-made pattern weaving around the trunks of the trees. Fencing. Most likely wrought-iron. It twisted and looped in fancy ornamentation. Beyond it, she saw even terraced rows of classically hewn tombstones fashioned in varying shapes and sizes. As she drew closer, she saw that many of the stones had bas-reliefs of the deceased.

She reached the fence. It only went up to her waist. She peered down its length to see if she could spot a gate. There wasn't one, at least not one she saw. "Well, it worked for the gate to the house," she concluded as she climbed over the fence.

With both feet on the other side, she surveyed the cemetery. She felt surrounded by graves. She had no idea where to begin. She thought back to the vision.

THE HAUNTING OF BLACKSTONE MANSION

"We didn't walk far, so she must be among these first two or three rows. Maybe even the first."

She started down the row. She read each grave's name: Herbert Blackstone, Elizabeth Blackstone, Edward Blackstone. She doubted that Eileen was buried in any of them. "What was the name?" She tried to recall that detail from the vision. "Marcus had said the cemetery. His great-grandfather. Gloria said..." She passed Donald Blackstone, Pearl Blackstone. "Gloria said..."

Silas Blackstone.

Katherine froze in her tracks. The face in the bas-relief was none other than the one she'd seen that first day in the mansion. The one carved onto the bust that was tucked away in the west-east hallway niche.

"Silas Blackstone," she reminded the tombstone. *This is the one! This is where Eileen's buried!*

She looked over the ground. She saw no sign that it had ever been disturbed. She scraped her foot along the soil. "It was shallow. They dumped her in a shallow grave." She looked down at her hands, which, tragically, were free of a shovel. She curled her fingers into claws. She pointed them at the grave's dirt. "Well, better get to it."

She got down on her hands and knees and clawed away dirt from the general area where her vision had shown her Eileen's head would be. In only a few seconds, she'd dug a few inches, but there was no sign of Eileen's remains. There was, in fact, no sign of anything other than more dirt.

She widened her hole. *Maybe she wasn't buried exactly where I thought.* She still came up with nothing. She dug farther down. Now to a full foot.

Scraping away a large clot of dirt, she came upon a tiny scrap of cloth. She picked it out. It was woven. She couldn't tell much detail in such a small sample, but she did see traces of florid details in gold and crimson. "The tablecloth?" *They carried her out of the house. Must've done it in this.*

She excitedly dug deeper all around the area where she'd found the scrap. Others appeared. Soon she'd gathered a small pile to the side of the grave.

But there was no sign of Eileen's remains.

She's gotta be here! She dug and dug. In another few minutes, she'd reached two feet, but the grave had long since stopped offering any more rotted tablecloth scraps.

She sat up. She dug the chunks of dirt out from under her fingernails. "Doesn't make any sense. If she's not here, where the hell is she?" She stood and informed the partially desecrated grave. "Even after a hundred years, there'd still be bones. And if not, why did she show me this?"

THE HAUNTING OF BLACKSTONE MANSION

She looked back up the hill at the mansion. "Why here? No, she didn't show me here. That was just the last thing she saw. She showed me... the tower!"

She haphazardly kicked the dirt and tablecloth scrap back into Silas's grave. She jumped over the fence and ran as fast as she could back up the hill to the mansion's entrance.

Inside, she took out and clicked on her flashlight, bolted through the entryway, and down the hallways to the west tower.

Reaching precisely where Eileen's ghost had left her, she pointed her flashlight down at the gunk she'd spewed when she'd awoken from the vision.

It was a big, pulpy mess. "Great. Gonna have to clean that up if we ever do anything with this place." She paused. "All right, Eileen, what did you want me to find?" She scanned the floorboards, but found nothing out of the ordinary. "Wait a minute." She bent down. "I wonder." She stood and scraped most of the vomit away with her shoe, then crouched down again.

There was a tiny gap between the floorboards upon which she'd emptied her stomach. Within it she saw a sliver of the same black as the cobblestone road that led to the mansion. "I wonder."

She stood. "Eileen! You got a hammer or crowbar or something?"

Eileen didn't answer.

"That's fine! I'll take it from here!" She marched down the hallway toward the heart of the house. "Gotta be something." She opened the first door, went inside, and gave the room a good 360 with her flashlight. Halfway through her turn, the beam landed on a fireplace. "Bingo."

She returned to the spot into which Eileen's ghost had thrust her head. She set her flashlight on its side on one of the spiral staircase's steps. The light shone roughly in the direction of where Eileen had left her. She stabbed a fire poker into the gap. She yanked and yanked. Soon, the board started to split away. Excited, she grabbed it, and tore it up.

She repeated the process with the next board and now had a hole in the floorboards directly above a surface of solid black stone masonry. Shining the flashlight on the masonry, she nodded with satisfaction.

She kicked the area. It held firm. "Can't just pick that out with a poker." She shone her flashlight in the direction of the front doors. "But I bet I know someone who can."

22

Katherine tore down the road as fast as she could. She kept an eye out for cops, but wasn't especially concerned about them right now. She was on her phone waiting for Kirk to pick up, but getting nothing but ringing. Voicemail finally came on.

"This is Kirk. After the beep, do what you gotta do. Later."

"Kirk! It's Kat! Listen, I've got a job. It's way more intense, may last a lot longer, but it'll pay a whole hell of a lot more. Round up your boys and gimme a call. Later." She hung up, placed her phone in its mount, and put on some good old bluegrass.

Reaching Blackstone, she slowed down as much as she needed to in order to keep Johnny Law off her back. She drove straight for the diner.

Wendy greeted her with a smile, "Kat! How the hell are ya?"

"Wendy, great to see you. I need a bloody steak, some hot cocoa, and the strongest stuff you can legally sell me."

Wendy nodded, very impressed. "Comin' right up, hon."

Katherine sat and called Jordan. His line also rang a bunch and finally went to voicemail.

He spoke in an atrociously offensive faux Black accent. "Yo, yo, yo! You got JB! Slap me wit' dem digits!"

Katherine rolled her eyes so hard she actually thought they might fall right out of her head. Despite her disgust, she maintained her polite demeanor. "Jordan, it's Kat. Listen, you have got a lot more in that house than a pile of old furniture. And it is gonna cost you to move. Gimme a ring." She hung up.

Wendy placed a mug of cocoa and a large shot glass full of gorgeous amber liquid in front of her. "Bon appétit."

Katherine lifted up the shot glass. "This whiskey?"

"Private stash. Looked like you needed it."

"Keep 'em coming."

"Not if you plan on drivin', kiddo."

Katherine nodded, then downed the shot.

Wendy leaned into her. "By the way. Sorry about Drew. I always thought he was a dick."

"Why didn't you warn me?"

Wendy stood. "You needed a place."

"Guess so."

"Need another one?"

THE HAUNTING OF BLACKSTONE MANSION

"Not at the moment, but soon, yeah."

"I'll ask around."

"Thanks."

Wendy soon brought her food. Katherine dug in.

She was only a third of the way through when her phone buzzed. She checked it. Kirk. "Hey, hey!"

"Got your message. What's up?"

"You are not gonna believe this. When you're done with work, come out to my motel. I'll tell you all about it."

"Sure, I can do that."

"I'll text you the address."

"That'd be useful."

"Just one question, Kirk."

"What's that?"

"Can you get your hands on a jackhammer?"

There was a brief pause. "I'll make some calls."

"You do that. See you soon."

After she was done with her meal at the diner, Katherine picked up some snacks at the store, though this time she skipped the tequila, and then returned to her motel room.

She was watching some trashy reality show when she heard a knock on her door. "Open."

Kirk walked in. "Nice."

Katherine grinned at him and scoffed. "In your face."

Kirk pretended to admire the room. "No, it's got a certain rustic quality."

"Have a seat." She got up and sat on the bed.

He took her seat. "So, a jackhammer?"

"Can you get one?"

"That's not really the question."

"Um, yes it is. It's kinda necessary. Unless you have access to a bigger tool."

"No, the question is why do you need that kind of machinery?"

"If I told you the whole story, you'd never believe me."

"Even after everything else you've told me?"

"This is a little different."

"Fair enough. I won't pry. Are we gonna be in any danger?"

"Other than the jackhammer, I can't imagine any, no."

"Good so far. How much? You said over the phone—"

"How much you want?"

"How much you offering?"

"How's double last time?"

"I mean..."

"Fine. Triple."

"Since when did you hit the jackpot?"

THE HAUNTING OF BLACKSTONE MANSION

"Not my jackpot. This is Jordan's."

"So this is the mansion again?"

"Yeah."

"Wait. We're digging up something at the actual mansion?"

"Yep."

"Is it, like, a treasure chest or something?"

She chuckled. "Not exactly."

"Kat, I don't know. This is sounding really..."

"Triple the pay, no danger, totally legit. I've got the paperwork. You in or not?"

"When do you need this done?"

"As soon as possible."

"I dunno if I can get guys together until at least tomorrow."

"Kirk, please."

"I'll make some calls." He stood. "Can we meet you there in, like, two hours?"

She stood too. "If you think you can get your equipment and guys over, then yeah. No time like the present."

"Great. I'll call if we hit any snags."

"Thanks, Kirk."

He smiled and started on his way out. "Listen, Kat, about the other night—"

"It's fine, Kirk. You were right. I probably do need time."

"I'm sorry I ghosted you."

AUGUSTINE PIERCE

"You didn't exactly ghost me."
"I was kinda planning on it."
She laughed. "Well, I'm glad you didn't."
"See you up there in two hours."
"See you then, Kirk."
He gave her a quick, polite nod and left.

Katherine met Kirk and his guys at Blackstone mansion's gate. "'Afternoon, boys!"

They all wished her the same.

"Lookin' good, Kat," Dennis said.

"Feelin' better?" Randy asked.

"I am," Katherine said. "Thank you, Randy."

"Ready to bust it up?" Shane pointed to the jackhammer in the back of his truck.

"You have no idea how ready."

"Shall we have at it, then?" Kirk asked.

"What are you British now?" Shane spoke in a crappy accent. "Bloody wanker."

The guys started moving the lights, generator, and jackhammer. As they headed up the hill, Katherine sidled up next to Kirk. She asked quietly, "We needed all four of you?"

"One to bust it open, two to carry away the chunks."

"And what will you be doing?"

THE HAUNTING OF BLACKSTONE MANSION

"Supervising," Kirk said with a smile.

"Seriously? Four?"

Kirk shrugged. "They're my boys."

Katherine led them into the mansion, through the entryway, into the hallway that led to the west tower, and finally to the place where she'd pulled up the boards.

Shane shone a light on the spot. "What the hell happened here?" He pointed at the dry vomit.

"Uh, nothing, just a little sick," Katherine said.

"That where I'm going?" Shane still pointed.

"Yep."

"Let's set up the lights," Kirk said.

He and the guys put up two lights on either side of the room. After Katherine took a second to let her eyes adjust, the first thing she saw was the triangular pattern. *Can't forget about that. Wonder if they've noticed it.* She looked briefly at each of their faces. None of them seemed to have seen it. One less thing she'd have to explain.

"All right, boys, time to suit up." Shane prepared the jackhammer and his safety clothes.

"Let's give him some space," Kirk said.

Katherine, Randy, and Dennis followed him out. Exiting the mansion, they heard Shane let the jackhammer rip.

Katherine asked Kirk, "How long's it gonna take?"

He shrugged. "A few hours. You got someplace to be?"

She shook her head. "Just curious."

He walked her a little ways down the hill. "So, you planning on staying?"

"You want me to stay?"

"Just curious."

"Well, if there's one thing I love to do, it's satisfy your curiosity, Kirk Whitehead. Yes, for the time being, I am planning to stay."

"You're not gonna hang out in that motel room forever, are you?"

"I've found a few leads. Jordan offered to help, and Wendy from the diner offered to help."

"That's a lot of help."

"Yeah, it's all right."

"If you like, I can also make a few calls."

"That'd be awfully sweet of you."

"That's me, Awful Sweet Kirk."

She laughed at their increasing silliness.

The jackhammer fell silent.

"What happened?" Katherine asked the group.

"Probably has a chunk or two for us to clear out," Randy said.

The group headed in, and sure enough, they found a very sweaty Shane standing next to a large pile of busted up rocks and mortar. Katherine took a close look at the hole he'd dug. It was only a

THE HAUNTING OF BLACKSTONE MANSION

few inches deep, but by the looks of it, unless the Blackstones had buried Eileen several feet down, this wasn't going to take that long.

Katherine, Kirk, Randy, and Dennis all carried some debris out to the front and dumped it onto the road.

Time passed by slowly for Katherine. She was so desperate to bust Eileen's remains out of there, but she knew Kirk's guys were professionals.

She and the guys chatted and played word games. Kirk patted a set of rocks like drums, and they even played a little I Spy to pass the time between loads of rocks and mortar. Finally, after another two hours, after they heard the jackhammer stop, they then heard Shane.

"What in the hell?!" he asked.

There she is. She and the guys ran into the house. They found a very freaked-out Shane hovering over the hole he'd dug.

He looked up at Katherine. "What the hell is this?"

"Chill, Shane. It's fine."

"It's not fine! There's a frickin' dead frickin' skeleton in there!" Shane pointed down.

"What?" Kirk joined him at the hole, then stared up at Katherine, but said nothing.

"Lemme see." Randy joined the other two.

"Ah, now I gotta see." Dennis joined the others.

"Did *you* do this?" Shane asked.

"Yes, Shane," Katherine deadpanned. "I murdered her over a century ago, tore up the floor all by myself, buried her, filled in all the masonry, then called you guys to dig her up because I finally felt like confessing."

Randy and Dennis gawked at each other as if they kind of believed her.

Kirk marched to her. "A minute?" He left the room.

She followed him into the hallway.

He closed the doors behind them and faced her. "You didn't tell me we'd find a body."

"I didn't know."

"But you suspected?"

She opened her mouth to answer, but didn't know what to say.

"Is it her?" he asked. "The one you saw in the attic?"

Katherine nodded.

He nodded slowly, likely weighing how annoyed or even pissed he was with her. He sighed. "All right. Let's do this." He opened the doors.

"Why's it all shiny?" Randy asked.

"What do you mean 'shiny'?" Katherine asked.

Randy answered as she joined them, "Shiny, like sparkly like a mirror."

Katherine peered into the hole. The jagged edges of torn-away rock opened up like a monster's wide, fang-lined maw into cool darkness. At the bottom there sat a lidless concrete coffin. Within it lay Eileen Byrne's softly illuminated remains.

Katherine took out her phone and tapped on its flashlight. The guys were completely silent as she traced the edge of the coffin with the phone's beam. The work was flawless. It rivaled any royal tomb. Whoever had created it was highly skilled, likely the greatest craftsman of his day.

She then shone the beam over the body. As Shane had complained, it was mostly bones. Quite a lot of hair remained, dangling from the skull, with strands swaying gently in a breeze that Katherine could neither feel nor hear. From the crown down to the top of the nasal cavity the skull was completely crushed. Terrible, vicious cracks were still visible in what was left of the eye sockets where Marcus had attacked. Some desiccated tissue still clung tightly to the skull's fiercely grinning visage, edges of ribs, limb bones, and joints.

Also, as Randy had observed, the bones were lying on what looked like a mirror. If Katherine wasn't mistaken, it was fashioned from the finest silver, the quality of its craftsmanship equal to that of the coffin's.

She nodded slowly. This corpse was the version that Eileen's ghost had shown her during their second encounter.

"What is it?" Kirk asked.

Katherine didn't lift her eyes from Eileen's remains. "Nothing."

She paused her phone's beam on a blade laid on top of the rib cage. Brown streaks, the remains of Eileen's dried blood, still clung to it. Katherine immediately recognized it as none other than the intended murder weapon, the cake knife.

"What's that?" Randy pointed.

"Looks like some kind of knife," Kirk said.

"It's a cake knife," Katherine filled them in.

"What's a cake knife?" Shane asked.

"It's a knife for cutting cakes. A luxury item."

Shane crouched and reached into the hole.

"Don't touch it!" Katherine warned.

Shane looked up at her as if to ask "Why the hell not?"

"It's a crime scene," Kirk said.

"That's right"—Katherine turned off her phone's flashlight and put the phone away—"and now I'm gonna walk down the hill and call the police. You guys did an excellent job. Once I'm done with the cops, we'll drive into town, and I'll get you paid." She headed toward the front doors.

"Kat?" Kirk asked.

She stopped and turned around. "Yeah?"

His face was clouded with confusion.

"Walk with me," she said.

THE HAUNTING OF BLACKSTONE MANSION

He waited till they'd left the mansion. "How did you know she was there?"

"She told me."

"What?"

"Well, technically, she didn't say anything, but she did show me."

He touched her shoulders. "Wait, stop."

Come on, Kirk. Just throw me down right here! "Told you you wouldn't believe me."

"I believe what I just saw in there. Why is there a cake knife in the hole with her? Why's she in a stone coffin? What's that mirror... thing?"

"Where do you want me to start?"

"The knife."

"Murder weapon."

"Her killer bust open the top of her head with a frickin' cake knife?"

"No. First, they attacked her and *thought* they killed her with the knife, but when they went to bury her out there in the family cemetery"—she pointed off to the west—"they realized she wasn't dead, so finished her off with a shovel."

"Slow down. 'They'? 'Family cemetery'?"

"First, her fiancé, then her fiancé's brother. They first buried her in a shallow grave on top of another grave—I dunno, that part wasn't clear—but obviously at some point, they exhumed her, and put her in there." She pointed at the mansion.

AUGUSTINE PIERCE

"Why would they do that? How do you know that?"

"I don't know and I told you, she showed me."

"So the coffin, what about that? And the mirror?"

She shook her head, just as baffled as he was. "Wish I knew."

"Doesn't make any sense. Why would they build her such an elaborate tomb, inside the house, when they'd murdered her?"

"You're right. It doesn't make any sense."

"I think I gotta sit down."

"I'll be right back."

"No, no, I'm coming with, but this is... a lot to take in."

"How do you think I've been feeling?"

They headed down the hill.

"I can't believe you saw her gh..." He trailed off.

"It was hard for me to say at first too."

"So, what happens now? You call the police; they recover the body; they bury her, where? Does she have any living relatives? Once it's all done and she has a proper burial, does she get to, you know, move on?"

"Where you want me to start?"

"Burial."

"I dunno where. Guess we'll figure that out. I dunno if she'll get to move on. I hope so. Oh, and the police have to do a DNA test."

"Right. To track down her relatives."

"Yeah, and hopefully an autopsy will confirm her pregnancy."

"Confirm her... Oh boy."

"I know, Kirk. I know." She took his arm, and they walked the rest of the way to the gate in silence.

Several yards down the road, once she was able to get some signal, she called 9-1-1. A half hour later, state troopers and a homicide team arrived, and before Katherine knew it, Eileen's body was being wheeled out.

Once the police had gotten Katherine's, Kirk's, and the other guys' statements, she returned to town with Kirk and the guys, paid them, and they said their goodbyes.

"Keep me posted. I wanna pay my respects," Kirk said.

"I will," Katherine said.

They all went their separate ways. She returned to the motel, and as she walked in, she called Jordan.

"Kat! What's all this about a hefty bill?"

"You seated, Jordan?"

"Uh, yeah, why?"

"This is gonna take a sec."

Weeks later, after the authorities had performed an autopsy on Eileen's remains, which did confirm a first-trimester pregnancy, they located one living relative, a several times great-niece, Josie, who was thirty-three years old and a married mother of three who lived in Oregon City, a suburb of Portland. With her family's participation, the state authorities arranged a formal funeral in Josie's town, about a half hour west of Blackstone.

Katherine, Kirk, his guys, Jordan, the officers who'd responded to Katherine's initial call, Josie, and her family all attended.

At the appropriate time, when the coffin was about to descend into the earth, Katherine placed the cake stand on the lid above approximately where Eileen's hands lay inside. Katherine figured that Reginald's engagement gift to her, though later so tainted, belonged with her.

As for the corresponding cake knife, after the police had returned it to Jordan, Katherine had requested it to keep as a reminder of what Eileen had been through.

After the service, the officers were the first to leave. Katherine thanked Josie and her family. Josie asked Katherine how she was ever able to discover Eileen's remains.

"It's a long story," Katherine said. "Let's just say I had a hunch."

THE HAUNTING OF BLACKSTONE MANSION

"Look, Kat, I got a thing, but let's check in later about the rest of the house." Jordan approached her by the side of Eileen's grave.

"Talk to you soon, Jordan."

Randy, Dennis, and Shane took their leave, which left Kirk and Katherine.

"So, I was thinking," Kirk began as he approached her.

"Sounds dangerous," she teased.

"Now that this is all over, I would love to finally take you out to dinner. For real."

Katherine felt the tiniest chill at the back of her neck. She turned around. Behind a nearby tree, she saw Eileen step out into the open. She looked the way Katherine had seen her in the photograph of the Blackstone gala, so happy and proud.

Eileen offered a shy wave.

Katherine kept her focus on her. "I'd love that, Kirk."

"Do you see her?"

Katherine nodded.

"How's she look?" he asked.

"I think she's gonna be just fine." Katherine waved back at Eileen.

Eileen smiled, then suddenly peered down to her left as if someone were calling her, though Katherine neither saw nor heard anything at all. Eileen looked back and mouthed something that seemed like "Gotta go." She offered one final wave and smiled wide.

Katherine smiled back.

Eileen turned away, toward the midday sun, walked off, and faded into nothing.

I wonder if that's how Dean would look if he were still hanging around. Wait. Could he be...?

She faced Mt. Hood from here, so many miles away, and though she couldn't see it, she knew Blackstone mansion, in its perpetual twilight woods, still held so many more dark secrets, though what those secrets were, she didn't yet know. "But this is all far from over."

The story continues in book two,
THE POSSESSION OF BLACKSTONE MANSION.
Start reading now!

The Possession of Blackstone Mansion

Some spirits only want to terrorize the living...

When Katherine prepares the mansion for the sale of its antiques, a new spirit contacts her from outside the house's dark and dusty halls.

This ghost is darker. More vicious. And it seems to find her everywhere.

As Katherine seeks to understand what the spirit needs, she finds an ancient and mysterious occult symbol, only the first clue in a much larger mystery.

But that's not all that possesses Blackstone mansion. She soon discovers a series of hidden tombs that contain the remains of the last generation to inhabit it.

If she doesn't unravel the truth soon, she may find there's a tomb waiting for her.

Start reading now!

Get your free book, *Zoe's Haunt*, by joining Augustine Pierce's newsletter. You can unsubscribe at any time.

Acknowledgments

First, thanks to my cover designers at MiblArt, who created a fantastic cover.

Also, thanks to my editor and proofreader, Paula.

DARK REALM

The Blackstone Trilogy

The Haunting of Blackstone Mansion
The Possession of Blackstone Mansion
The Fall of Blackstone Mansion

Also by Augustine Pierce

The Curse of Braddock Mansion

Horror in Paradise

Cenote

Arena

Down

About the Author

Augustine Pierce is the author of *The Curse of Braddock Mansion, Cenote, Zoe's Haunt, Arena, Down, The Haunting of Blackstone Mansion, The Possession of Blackstone Mansion,* and *The Fall of Blackstone Mansion*. He lives in Paris with his wife and collection of horror board games. He enjoys travel, snorkeling, and all things macabre.

Stay in touch! Subscribe to Augustine Pierce's newsletter and follow his Facebook page!

authoraugustinepierce@gmail.com

Printed in Great Britain
by Amazon